wife. When he came around and coughed under our tree, father laughed at him and threw rocks at him. It was our way in those days. We did not know how to add strength together and become strong."

"Would a brother take a brother's wife?" Deer-Runner demanded.

"Yes, if he had gone to live in another tree by himself."

"But we do not do such things now," Afraid-of-the-Dark objected.

"It is because I have taught your fathers better." Long-Beard thrust his hairy paw into the bear meat and drew out a handful of suet, which he sucked with a meditative air. Again he wiped his hands on his naked sides and went on. "What I am telling you happened in the long ago, before we knew any better."

"You must have been fools not to know better," was Deer-Runner's comment, Yellow-Head grunting approval.

"So we were, but we became bigger fools, as you shall see. Still, we did learn better, and this was the way of it. We Fish-Eaters had not learned to add our strength until our strength was the strength of all of us. But the Meat-Eaters, who lived across the divide in the Big Valley, stood together, hunted together, fished together, and fought together. One day they came into our valley. Each family of us got into its own cave and tree. There were only ten Meat-Eaters, but they fought together, and we fought, each family by itself."

Long-Beard counted long and perplexedly on his fingers.

"There were sixty men of us," was what he managed to say with fingers and lips combined. "And we were very strong, only we did not know it. So we watched the ten men attack Boo-oogh's tree. He made a good fight, but he had no chance. We looked on. When some of the Meat-Eaters tried to climb the tree, Boo-oogh had to show himself in order to drop stones on their heads, whereupon the other Meat-Eaters, who were waiting for that very thing, shot him full of arrows. And that was the end of Boo-oogh.

"Next, the Meat-Eaters got One-Eye and his family in his cave. They built a fire in the mouth and smoked him out, like we smoked out the bear there to-day. Then they went after Six-Fingers, up his tree, and, while they were killing him and his grown son, the rest of us ran away. They caught some of our women, and killed two old men who could not run fast and several children. The women they carried away with them to the Big Valley.

"After that the rest of us crept back, and, somehow, perhaps because we were in fear and felt the need for one another, we talked the thing over. It was our first council, our first real council. And in that council we formed our first tribe. For we had learned the lesson. Of the ten Meat-Eaters, each man had had the strength of ten, for the ten had fought as one man. They had added their strength together. But of the thirty families and the sixty men of us, we had had the strength of but one man, for each had fought alone.

"It was a great talk we had, and it was hard talk, for we did not have the words then as now with which to talk. The Bug made some of the words long afterward, and so did others of us make words from time to time. But in the end we agreed to add our strength together and to be as one man when the Meat-Eaters came over the divide to steal our women. And that was the tribe.

"We set two men on the divide, one for the day and one for the night, to watch if the Meat-Eaters came. These were the eyes of the tribe. Then, also, day and night, there were to be ten men awake with their clubs and spears and arrows in their hands, ready to fight. Before, when a man went after fish, or clams, or gull-eggs, he carried his weapons with him, and half the time he was getting food and half the time watching for fear some other man would get him. Now that was all changed. The men went out without their weapons and spent all their time getting food. Likewise, when the women went into the mountains after roots and berries, five of the ten men went with them to guard them. While all the time, day and night, the eyes of the tribe watched from the top of the divide.

"But troubles came. As usual, it was about the women. Men without wives wanted other men's wives, and there was much fighting between men, and now and again one got his head smashed or a spear through his body. While one of the watchers was on top of the divide, another man stole his wife, and he came down to fight. Then the other watcher was in fear that some one would take his wife, and he came down likewise. Also, there was trouble among the ten men who carried always their weapons, and they fought five against five, till some ran away down the coast and the others ran after them.

"So it was that the tribe was left without eyes or guards. We had not the strength of sixty. We had no strength at all. So we held a council and made our first laws. I was but a cub at the time, but I remember. We said that, in order to be strong, we must not fight one another, and we made a law that when a man killed another him would the tribe kill. We made another law that whoso stole another man's wife him would the tribe kill. We said that whatever man had too great strength, and by that strength hurt his brothers in the tribe, him would we kill that his strength might hurt no more. For, if we let his strength hurt, the brothers would become afraid and the tribe would fall apart, and we would be as weak as when the Meat-Eaters first came upon us and killed Boo-oogh.

"Knuckle-Bone was a strong man, a very strong man, and he knew not law. He knew only his own strength, and in the fullness thereof he went forth and took the wife of Three-Clams. Three-Clams tried to fight, but Knuckle-Bone clubbed out his brains. Yet had Knuckle-Bone forgotten that all the men of us had added our strength to keep the law among us, and him we killed, at the foot of his tree, and hung his body on a branch as a warning that the law was stronger than any man. For we were the law, all of us, and no man was greater than the law.

"Then there were other troubles, for know, O Deer-Runner, and Yellow-Head, and Afraid-of-the-Dark, that it is not easy to make a tribe. There were many things, little things, that it was a great trouble to call all the men together to have a council about. We were having councils morning, noon, and night, and in the middle of the night. We could find little time to go out and get food, because of the councils, for there was always some little thing to be settled, such as naming two new watchers to take the place of the old ones on the hill, or naming how much food should fall to the share of the men who kept their weapons always in their hands and got no food for themselves.

"We stood in need of a chief man to do these things, who would be the voice of the council, and who would account to the council for the things he did. So we named Fith-Fith the chief man. He was a strong man, too, and very cunning, and when he was angry he made noises just like that, fith-fith, like a wild-cat.

"The ten men who guarded the tribe were set to work making a wall of stones across the narrow part of the valley. The women and large children helped, as did other men, until the wall was strong. After that, all the families came down out of their caves and trees and built grass houses behind the shelter of the wall. These houses were large and much better than the caves and trees, and everybody had a better time of it because the men had added their strength together and become a tribe. Because of the wall and the guards and the watchers, there was more time to hunt and fish and pick roots and berries; there was more food, and better food, and no one went hungry. And Three-Legs, so named because his legs had been smashed when a boy and who walked with a stick— Three-Legs got the seed of the wild corn and planted it in the ground in the valley near his house. Also, he tried planting fat roots and other things he found in the mountain valleys.

"Because of the safety in the Sea Valley, which was because of the wall and the watchers and the guards, and because there was food in plenty for all without having to fight for it, many families came in from the coast valleys on both sides and from the high back mountains where they had lived more like wild animals than men. And it was not long before the Sea Valley filled up, and in it were countless families. But, before this happened, the land, which had been free to all and belonged to all, was divided up. Three-Legs began it when he planted corn. But most of us did not care about the land. We thought the marking of the boundaries with fences of stone was a foolishness. We had plenty to eat, and what more did we want? I remember that my father and I built stone fences for Three-Legs and were given corn in return.

"So only a few got all the land, and Three-Legs got most of it. Also, others that had taken land gave it to the few that held on, being paid in return with corn and fat roots, and bear-skins, and fishes which the farmers got from the fishermen in exchange for corn. And, the first thing we knew, all the land was gone.

"It was about this time that Fith-Fith died and Dog-Tooth, his son, was made chief. He demanded to be made chief anyway, because his father had been chief before him. Also, he looked upon himself as a greater chief than his father. He was a good chief at first, and worked hard, so that the council had less and less to do. Then arose a new voice in the Sea Valley. It was Twisted-Lip. We had never thought much of him, until he began to talk with the spirits of the dead. Later we called him Big-Fat, because he ate over-much, and did no work, and grew round and large. One day Big-Fat told us that the secrets of the dead were his, and that he was the voice of God. He became great friends with Dog-Tooth, who commanded that we should build Big-Fat a grass house. And Big-Fat put taboos all around this house and kept God inside.

"More and more Dog-Tooth became greater than the council, and when the council grumbled and said it would name a new chief, Big-Fat spoke with the voice of God and said no. Also, Three-Legs and the others who held the land stood behind Dog-Tooth. Moreover, the strongest man in the council was Sea-Lion, and him the land-owners gave land to secretly, along with many bearskins and baskets of corn. So Sea-Lion said that Big-Fat's voice was truly the voice of God and must be obeyed. And soon afterward Sea-Lion was named the voice of Dog-Tooth and did most of his talking for him.

"Then there was Little-Belly, a little man, so thin in the middle that he looked as if he had never had enough to eat. Inside the mouth of the river, after the sand-bar had combed the strength of the breakers, he built a big fish-trap. No man had ever seen or dreamed a fish-trap before. He worked weeks on it, with his son and his wife, while the rest of us laughed at their labours. But, when it was done, the first day he caught more fish in it than could the whole tribe in a week, whereat there was great rejoicing. There was only one other place in the river for a fish-trap, but, when my father and I and a dozen other men started to make a very large trap, the guards came from the big grass-house we had built for Dog-Tooth. And the guards poked us with their spears and told us begone, because Little-Belly was going to build a trap there himself on the word of Sea-Lion, who was the voice of Dog-Tooth.

"There was much grumbling, and my father called a council. But, when he rose to speak, him the Sea-Lion thrust through the throat with a spear and he died. And Dog-Tooth and Little-Belly, and Three-Legs and all that held land said it was good. And Big-Fat said it was the will of God. And after that all men were afraid to stand up in the council, and there was no more council.

"Another man, Pig-Jaw, began to keep goats. He had heard about it as among the Meat-Eaters, and it was not long before he had many flocks. Other men, who had no land and no fish-traps, and who else would have gone hungry, were glad to work for Pig-Jaw, caring for his goats, guarding them from wild dogs and tigers, and driving them to the feeding pastures in the mountains. In return, Pig-Jaw gave them goat-meat to eat and goat-skins to wear, and sometimes they traded the goat-meat for fish and corn and fat roots.

"It was this time that money came to be. Sea-Lion was the man who first thought of it, and he talked it over with Dog-Tooth and Big-Fat. You see, these three were the ones that got a share of everything in the Sea Valley. One basket out of every three of corn was theirs, one fish out of every three, one goat out of every three. In return, they fed the guards and the watchers, and kept the rest for themselves. Sometimes, when a big haul of fish was made they did not know what to do with all their share. So Sea-Lion set the women to making money out of shell, little round pieces, with a hole in each one, and all made smooth and fine. These were strung on strings, and the strings were called money.

"Each string was of the value of thirty fish, or forty fish, but the women, who made a string a day, were given two fish each. The fish came out of the shares of Dog-Tooth, Big-Fat, and Sea-Lion, which they three did not eat. So all the money belonged to them. Then they told Three-Legs and the other land-owners that they would take their share of corn and roots in money, Little-Belly that they would take their share of fish in money, Pig-Jaw that they would take their share of goats and cheese in money. Thus, a man who had nothing, worked for one who had, and was paid in money. With this money he bought corn, and fish, and meat, and cheese. And Three-Legs and all owners of things paid Dog-Tooth and Sea-Lion and Big-Fat their share in money. And they paid the guards and watchers in money, and the guards and watchers bought their food with the money. And, because money was cheap, Dog-Tooth made many more men into guards. And, because money was cheap to make, a number of men began to make money out of shell themselves. But the guards stuck spears in them and shot them full of arrows, because they were trying to break up the tribe. It was bad to break up the tribe, for then the Meat-Eaters would come over the divide and kill them all.

"Big-Fat was the voice of God, but he took Broken-Rib and made him into a priest, so that he became the voice of Big-Fat and did most of his talking for him. And both had other men to be servants to them. So, also, did Little-Belly and Three-Legs and Pig-Jaw have other men to lie in the sun about their grass houses and carry messages for them and give commands. And more and more were men taken away from work, so that those that were left worked harder than ever before. It seemed that men desired to do no work and strove to seek out other ways whereby men should work for them. Crooked-Eyes found such a way. He made the first fire-brew out of corn. And thereafter he worked no more, for he talked secretly with Dog-Tooth and Big-Fat and the other masters, and it was agreed that he should be the only one to make fire-brew. But Crooked-Eyes did no work himself. Men made the brew for him, and he paid them in money. Then he sold the fire-brew for money, and all men bought. And many strings of money did he give Dog-Tooth and Sea-Lion and all of them.

"Big-Fat and Broken-Rib stood by Dog-Tooth when he took his second wife, and his third wife. They said Dog-Tooth was different from other men and second only to God that Big-Fat kept in his taboo house, and Dog-Tooth said so, too, and wanted to know who were they to grumble about how many wives he took. Dog-Tooth had a big canoe made, and, many more men he took from work, who did nothing and lay in the sun, save only when Dog-Tooth went in the canoe, when they paddled for him. And he made Tiger-Face head man over all the guards, so that Tiger-Face became his right arm, and when he did not like a man Tiger-Face killed that man for him. And Tiger-Face, also, made another man to be his right arm, and to give commands, and to kill for him.

"But this was the strange thing: as the days went by we who were left worked harder and harder, and yet did we get less and less to eat."

"But what of the goats and the corn and the fat roots and the fish-trap?" spoke up Afraid-of-the-Dark, "what of all this? Was there not more food to be gained by man's work?"

"It is so," Long-Beard agreed. "Three men on the fish-trap got more fish than the whole tribe before there was a fish-trap. But have I not said we were fools? The more food we were able to get, the less food did we have to eat."

"But was it not plain that the many men who did not work ate it all up?" Yellow-Head demanded.

Long-Beard nodded his head sadly.

"Dog-Tooth's dogs were stuffed with meat, and the men who lay in the sun and did no work were rolling in fat, and, at the same time, there were little children crying themselves to sleep with hunger biting them with every wail."

Deer-Runner was spurred by the recital of famine to tear out a chunk of bear-meat and broil it on a stick over the coals. This he devoured with smacking lips, while Long-Beard went on:

"When we grumbled Big-Fat arose, and with the voice of God said that God had chosen the wise men to own the land and the goats and the fish-trap, and the fire-brew, and that without these wise men we would all be animals, as in the days when we lived in trees.

"And there arose one who became a singer of songs for the king. Him they called the Bug, because he was small and ungainly of face and limb and excelled not in work or deed. He loved the fattest marrow bones, the choicest fish, the milk warm from the goats, the first corn that was ripe, and the snug place by the fire. And thus, becoming singer of songs to the king, he found a way to do nothing and be fat. And when the people grumbled more and more, and some threw stones at the king's grass house, the Bug sang a song of how good it was to be a Fish-Eater. In his song he told that the Fish-Eaters were the chosen of God and the finest men God had made. He sang of the Meat-Eaters as pigs and crows, and sang how fine and good it was for the Fish-Eaters to fight and die doing God's work, which was the killing of Meat-Eaters. The words of his song were like fire in us, and we clamoured to be led against the Meat-Eaters. And we forgot that we were hungry, and why we had grumbled, and were glad to be led by Tiger-Face over the divide, where we killed many Meat-Eaters and were content.

"But things were no better in the Sea Valley. The only way to get food was to work for Three-Legs or Little-Belly or Pig-Jaw; for there was no land that a man might plant with corn for himself. And often there were more men than Three-Legs and the others had work for. So these men went hungry, and so did their wives and children and their old mothers. Tiger-Face said they could become guards if they wanted to, and many of them did, and thereafter they did no work except to poke spears in the men who did work and who grumbled at feeding so many idlers.

"And when we grumbled, ever the Bug sang new songs. He said that Three-Legs and Pig-Jaw and the rest were strong men, and that that was why they had so much. He said that we should be glad to have strong men with us, else would we perish of our own worthlessness and the Meat-Eaters. Therefore, we should be glad to let such strong men have all they could lay hands on. And Big-Fat and Pig-Jaw and Tiger-Face and all the rest said it was true.

"'All right,' said Long-Fang, 'then will I, too, be a strong man.' And he got himself corn, and began to make fire-brew and sell it for strings of money. And, when Crooked-Eyes complained, Long-Fang said that he was himself a strong man, and that if Crooked-Eyes made any more noise he would bash his brains out for him. Whereat Crooked-Eyes was afraid and went and talked with Three-Legs and Pig-Jaw. And all three went and talked to Dog-Tooth. And Dog-Tooth spoke to Sea-Lion, and Sea-Lion sent a runner with a message to Tiger-Face. And Tiger-Face sent his guards, who burned Long-Fang's house along with the fire-brew he had made. Also, they killed him and all his family. And Big-Fat said it was good, and the Bug sang another song about how good it was to observe the law, and what a fine land the Sea Valley was, and how every man who loved the Sea Valley should go forth and kill the bad Meat-Eaters. And again his song was as fire to us, and we forgot to grumble.

"It was very strange. When Little-Belly caught too many fish, so that it took a great many to sell for a little money, he threw many of the fish back into the sea, so that more money would be paid for what was left. And Three-Legs often let many large fields lie idle so as to get more money for his corn. And the women, making so much money out of shell that much money was needed to buy with, Dog-Tooth stopped the making of money. And the women had no work, so they took the places of the men. I worked on the fish-trap, getting a string of money every five days. But my sister now did my work, getting a string of money for every ten days. The women worked cheaper, and there was less food, and Tiger-Face said we should become guards. Only I could not become a guard because I was lame of one leg and Tiger-Face would not have me. And there were many like me. We were broken men and only fit to beg for work or to take care of the babies while the women worked."

Yellow-Head, too, was made hungry by the recital and broiled a piece of bear-meat on the coals.

"But why didn't you rise up, all of you, and kill Three-Legs and Pig-Jaw and Big-Fat and the rest and get enough to eat?" Afraid-in-the-Dark demanded.

"Because we could not understand," Long-Beard answered. "There was too much to think about, and, also, there were the guards sticking spears into us, and Big-Fat talking about God, and the Bug singing new songs. And when any man did think right, and said so, Tiger-Face and the guards got him, and he was tied out to the rocks at low tide so that the rising waters drowned him.

"It was a strange thing—the money. It was like the Bug's songs. It seemed all right, but it wasn't, and we were slow to understand. Dog-Tooth began to gather the money in. He put it in a big pile, in a grass house, with guards to watch it day and night. And the more money he piled in the house the dearer money became, so that a man worked a longer time for a string of money than before. Then, too, there was always talk of war with the Meat-Eaters, and Dog-Tooth and Tiger-Face filled many houses with corn, and dried fish, and smoked goat-meat, and cheese. And with the food, piled there in mountains the people had not enough to eat. But what did it matter? Whenever the people grumbled too loudly the Bug sang a new song, and Big-Fat said it was God's word that we should kill Meat-Eaters, and Tiger-Face led us over the divide to kill and be killed. I was not good enough to be a guard and lie fat in the sun, but, when we made war, Tiger-Face was glad to take me along. And when we had eaten, all the food stored in the houses we stopped fighting and went back to work to pile up more food."

"Then were you all crazy," commented Deer-Runner.

"Then were we indeed all crazy," Long-Beard agreed. "It was strange, all of it. There was Split-Nose. He said everything was wrong. He said it was true that we grew strong by adding our strength together. And he said that, when we first formed the tribe, it was right that the men whose strength hurt the tribe should be shorn of their strength, men who bashed their brothers' heads and stole their brothers' wives. And now, he said, the tribe was not getting stronger, but was getting weaker, because there were men with another kind of strength that were hurting the tribe, men who had the strength of the land, like Three-Legs; who had the strength of the fish-trap, like Little-Belly; who had the strength of all the goat-meat, like Pig-Jaw. The thing to do, Split-Nose said, was to shear these men of their evil strength; to make them go to work, all of them, and to let no man eat who did not work.

"And the Bug sang another song about men like Split-Nose, who wanted to go back, and live in trees.

"Yet Split-Nose said no; that he did not want to go back, but ahead; that they grew strong only as they added their strength together; and that, if the Fish-Eaters would add their strength to the Meat-Eaters, there would be no more fighting and no more watchers and no more guards, and that, with all men working, there would be so much food that each man would have to work not more than two hours a day.

"Then the Bug sang again, and he sang that Split-Nose was lazy, and he sang also the 'Song of the Bees.' It was a strange song, and those who listened were made mad, as from the drinking of strong fire-brew. The song was of a swarm of bees, and of a robber wasp who had come in to live with the bees and who was stealing all their honey. The wasp was lazy and told them there was no need to work; also, he told them to make friends with the bears, who were not honey-stealers but only very good friends. And the Bug sang in crooked words, so that those who listened knew that the swarm was the Sea Valley tribe, that the bears were the Meat-Eaters, and that the lazy wasp was Split-Nose. And when the Bug sang that the bees listened to the wasp till the swarm was near to perishing, the people growled and snarled, and when the Bug sang that at last the good bees arose and stung the wasp to death, the people picked up stones from the ground and stoned Split-Nose to death till there was naught to be seen of him but the heap of stones they had flung on top of him. And there were many poor people who worked long and hard and had not enough to eat that helped throw the stones on Split-Nose.

"And, after the death of Split-Nose, there was but one other man that dared rise up and speak his mind, and that man was Hair-Face. 'Where is the strength of the strong?' he asked. 'We are the strong, all of us, and we are stronger than Dog-Tooth and Tiger-Face and Three-Legs and Pig-Jaw and all the rest who do nothing and eat much and weaken us by the hurt of their strength which is bad strength. Men who are slaves are not strong. If the man who first found the virtue and use of fire had used his strength we would have been his slaves, as we are the slaves to-day of Little-Belly, who found the virtue and use of the fish-trap; and of the men who found the virtue and use of the land, and the goats, and the fire-brew. Before, we lived in trees, my brothers, and no man was safe. But we fight no more with one another. We have added our strength together. Then let us fight no more with the Meat-Eaters. Let us add our strength and their strength together. Then will we be indeed strong. And then we will go out together, the Fish-Eaters and the Meat-Eaters, and we will kill the tigers and the lions and the wolves and the wild dogs, and we will pasture our goats on all the hill-sides and plant our corn and fat roots in all the high mountain valleys. In that day we will be so strong that all the wild animals will flee before us and perish. And nothing will withstand us, for the strength of each man will be the strength of all men in the world.'

"So said Hair-Face, and they killed him, because, they said, he was a wild man and wanted to go back and live in a tree. It was very strange. Whenever a man arose and wanted to go forward all those that stood still said he went backward and should be killed. And the poor people helped stone him, and were fools. We were all fools, except those who were fat and did no work. The fools were called wise, and the wise were stoned. Men who worked did not get enough to eat, and the men who did not work ate too much.

"And the tribe went on losing strength. The children were weak and sickly. And, because we ate not enough, strange sicknesses came among us and we died like flies. And then the Meat-Eaters came upon us. We had followed Tiger-Face too often over the divide and killed them. And now they came to repay in blood. We were too weak and sick to man the big wall. And they killed us, all of us, except some of the women, which they took away with them. The Bug and I escaped, and I hid in the wildest places, and became a hunter of meat and went hungry no more. I stole a wife from the Meat-Eaters, and went to live in the caves of the high mountains where they could not find me. And we had three sons, and each son stole a wife from the Meat-Eaters. And the rest you know, for are you not the sons of my sons?"

"But the Bug?" queried Deer-Runner. "What became of him?"

"He went to live with the Meat-Eaters and to be a singer of songs to the king. He is an old man now, but he sings the same old songs; and, when a man rises up to go forward, he sings that that man is walking backward to live in a tree."

Long-Beard dipped into the bear-carcass and sucked with toothless gums at a fist of suet.

"Some day," he said, wiping his hands on his sides, "all the fools will be dead and then all live men will go forward. The strength of the strong will be theirs, and they will add their strength together, so that, of all the men in the world, not one will fight with another. There will be no guards nor watchers on the walls. And all the hunting animals will be killed, and, as Hair-Face said, all the hill-sides will be pastured with goats and all the high mountain valleys will be planted with corn and fat roots. And all men will be brothers, and no man will lie idle in the sun and be fed by his fellows. And all that will come to pass in the time when the fools are dead, and when there will be no more singers to stand still and sing the 'Song of the Bees.' Bees are not men."

SOUTH OF THE SLOT

Old San Francisco, which is the San Francisco of only the other day, the day before the Earthquake, was divided midway by the Slot. The Slot was an iron crack that ran along the centre of Market Street, and from the Slot arose the burr of the ceaseless, endless cable that was hitched at will to the cars it dragged up and down. In truth, there were two slots, but in the quick grammar of the West time was saved by calling them, and much more that they stood for, "The Slot." North of the Slot were the theatres, hotels, and shopping district, the banks and the staid, respectable business houses. South of the Slot were the factories, slums, laundries, machine-shops, boiler works, and the abodes of the working class.

The Slot was the metaphor that expressed the class cleavage of Society, and no man crossed this metaphor, back and forth, more successfully than Freddie Drummond. He made a practice of living in both worlds, and in both worlds he lived signally well. Freddie Drummond was a professor in the

Sociology Department of the University of California, and it was as a professor of sociology that he first crossed over the Slot, lived for six mouths in the great labour-ghetto, and wrote The Unskilled Labourer, a book that was hailed everywhere as an able contribution to the literature of progress, and as a splendid reply to the literature of discontent. Politically and economically it was nothing if not orthodox. Presidents of great railway systems bought whole editions of it to give to their employees. The Manufacturers' Association alone distributed fifty thousand copies of it. In a way, it was almost as immoral as the far-famed and notorious Message to Garcia, while in its pernicious preachment of thrift and content it ran Mr. Wiggs of the Cabbage Patch a close second.

At first, Freddie Drummond found it monstrously difficult to get along among the working people. He was not used to their ways, and they certainly were not used to his. They were suspicious. He had no antecedents. He could talk of no previous jobs. His hands were soft. His extraordinary politeness was ominous. His first idea of the rôle he would play was that of a free and independent American who chose to work with his hands and no explanations given. But it wouldn't do, as he quickly discovered. At the beginning they accepted him, very provisionally, as a freak. A little later, as he began to know his way about better, he insensibly drifted into the rôle that would work— namely, he was a man who had seen better days, very much better days, but who was down on his luck, though, to be sure, only temporarily.

He learned many things, and generalized much and often erroneously, all of which can be found in the pages of The Unskilled Labourer. He saved himself, however, after the sane and conservative manner of his kind, by labelling his generalizations as "tentative." One of his first experiences was in the great Wilmax Cannery, where he was put on piece-work making small packing cases. A box factory supplied the parts, and all Freddie Drummond had to do was to fit the parts into a form and drive in the wire nails with a light hammer.

It was not skilled labour, but it was piece-work. The ordinary labourers in the cannery got a dollar and a half per day. Freddie Drummond found the other men on the same job with him jogging along and earning a dollar and seventy-five cents a day. By the third day he was able to earn the same. But he was ambitious. He did not care to jog along and, being unusually able and fit, on the fourth day earned two dollars.

The next day, having keyed himself up to an exhausting high-tension, he earned two dollars and a half. His fellow workers favoured him with scowls and black looks, and made remarks, slangily witty and which he did not understand, about sucking up to the boss and pace-making and holding her down, when the rains set in. He was astonished at their malingering on piece-work, generalized about the inherent laziness of the unskilled labourer, and proceeded next day to hammer out three dollars' worth of boxes.

And that night, coming out of the cannery, he was interviewed by his fellow workmen, who were very angry and incoherently slangy. He failed to comprehend the motive behind their action. The action itself was strenuous. When he refused to ease down his pace and bleated about freedom of contract, independent Americanism, and the dignity of toil, they proceeded to spoil his pace-making ability. It was a fierce battle, for Drummond was a large man and an athlete, but the crowd finally jumped on his ribs, walked on his face, and stamped on his fingers, so that it was only after lying in bed for a week that he was able to get up and look for another job. All of which is duly narrated in that first book of his, in the chapter entitled "The Tyranny of Labour."

A little later, in another department of the Wilmax Cannery, lumping as a fruit-distributor among the women, he essayed to carry two boxes of fruit at a time, and was promptly reproached by the other fruit-lumpers. It was palpable malingering; but he was there, he decided, not to change conditions, but to observe. So he lumped one box thereafter, and so well did he study the art of shirking that he wrote a special chapter on it, with the last several paragraphs devoted to tentative generalizations.

In those six months he worked at many jobs and developed into a very good imitation of a genuine worker. He was a natural linguist, and he kept notebooks, making a scientific study of the workers' slang or argot, until he could talk quite intelligibly. This language also enabled him more intimately to follow their mental processes, and thereby to gather much data for a projected chapter in some future book which he planned to entitle Synthesis of Working-Class Psychology.

Before he arose to the surface from that first plunge into the underworld he discovered that he was a good actor and demonstrated the plasticity of his nature. He was himself astonished at his own fluidity. Once having mastered the language and conquered numerous fastidious qualms, he found that he could flow into any nook of working-class life and fit it so snugly as to feel comfortably at home. As he said, in the preface to his second book, The Toiler, he endeavoured really to know the working people, and the only possible way to achieve this was to work beside them, eat their food, sleep in their beds, be amused with their amusements, think their thoughts, and feel their feeling.

He was not a deep thinker. He had no faith in new theories. All his norms and criteria were conventional. His Thesis on the French Revolution was noteworthy in college annals, not merely for its painstaking and voluminous accuracy, but for the fact that it was the dryest, deadest, most formal, and most orthodox screed ever written on the subject. He was a very reserved man, and his natural inhibition was large in quantity and steel-like in quality. He had but few friends. He was too undemonstrative, too frigid. He had no vices, nor had any one ever discovered any temptations. Tobacco he detested, beer he abhorred, and he was never known to drink anything stronger than an occasional light wine at dinner.

When a freshman he had been baptized "Ice-Box" by his warmer-blooded fellows. As a member of the faculty he was known as "Cold-Storage." He had but one grief, and that was "Freddie." He had earned it when he played full-back in the 'Varsity eleven, and his formal soul had never succeeded in living it down. "Freddie" he would ever be, except officially, and through nightmare vistas he looked into a future when his world would speak of him as "Old Freddie."

For he was very young to be a doctor of sociology, only twenty-seven, and he looked younger. In appearance and atmosphere he was a strapping big college man, smooth-faced and easy-mannered, clean and simple and wholesome, with a known record of being a splendid athlete and an implied vast possession of cold culture of the inhibited sort. He never talked shop out of class and committee rooms, except later on, when his books showered him with distasteful public notice and he yielded to the extent of reading occasional papers before certain literary and economic societies.

He did everything right, too right; and in dress and comportment was inevitably correct. Not that he was a dandy. Far from it. He was a college man, in dress and carriage as like as a pea to the type that of late years is being so generously turned out of our institutions of higher learning. His handshake was satisfyingly strong and stiff. His blue eyes were coldly blue and convincingly sincere. His voice, firm and masculine, clean and crisp of enunciation, was pleasant to the ear. The one drawback to Freddie Drummond was his inhibition. He never unbent. In his football days, the higher the tension of the game, the cooler he grew. He was noted as a boxer, but he was regarded as an automaton, with the inhuman precision of a machine judging distance and timing blows, guarding, blocking, and stalling. He was rarely punished himself, while he rarely punished an opponent. He was too clever and too controlled to permit himself to put a pound more weight into a punch than he intended. With him it was a matter of exercise. It kept him fit.

As time went by, Freddie Drummond found himself more frequently crossing the Slot and losing himself in South of Market. His summer and winter holidays were spent there, and, whether it was a week or a week-end, he found the time spent there to be valuable and enjoyable. And there was so much material to be gathered. His third book, Mass and Master, became a text-book in the American universities; and almost before he knew it, he was at work on a fourth one, The Fallacy of the Inefficient.

Somewhere in his make-up there was a strange twist or quirk. Perhaps it was a recoil from his environment and training, or from the tempered seed of his ancestors, who had been book-men generation preceding generation; but at any rate, he found enjoyment in being down in the working-class world. In his own world he was "Cold-Storage," but down below he was "Big" Bill Totts, who could drink and smoke, and slang and fight, and be an all-round favourite. Everybody liked Bill, and more than one working girl made love to him. At first he had been merely a good actor, but as time went on, simulation became second nature. He no longer played a part, and he loved sausages, sausages and bacon, than which, in his own proper sphere, there was nothing more loathsome in the way of food.

From doing the thing for the need's sake, he came to doing the thing for the thing's sake. He found himself regretting as the time drew near for him to go back to his lecture-room and his inhibition. And he often found himself waiting with anticipation for the dreamy time to pass when he could cross the Slot and cut loose and play the devil. He was not wicked, but as "Big" Bill Totts he did a myriad things that Freddie Drummond would never have been permitted to do. Moreover, Freddie Drummond never would have wanted to do them. That was the strangest part of his discovery. Freddie Drummond and Bill Totts were two totally different creatures. The desires and tastes and impulses of each ran counter to the other's. Bill Totts could shirk at a job with clear conscience, while Freddie Drummond condemned shirking as vicious, criminal, and un-American, and devoted whole chapters to condemnation of the vice. Freddie Drummond did not care for dancing, but Bill Totts never missed the nights at the various dancing clubs, such as The Magnolia, The Western Star, and The Elite; while he won a massive silver cup, standing thirty inches high, for being the best-sustained character at the Butchers and Meat Workers' annual grand masked ball. And Bill Totts liked the girls and the girls liked him, while Freddie Drummond enjoyed playing the ascetic in this particular, was open in his opposition to equal suffrage, and cynically bitter in his secret condemnation of coeducation.

Freddie Drummond changed his manners with his dress, and without effort. When he entered the obscure little room used for his transformation scenes, he carried himself just a bit too stiffly. He was too erect, his shoulders were an inch too far back, while his face was grave, almost harsh, and practically expressionless. But when he emerged in Bill Totts' clothes he was another creature. Bill Totts did not slouch, but somehow his whole form limbered up and became graceful. The very sound of the voice was changed, and the laugh was loud and hearty, while loose speech and an occasional oath were as a matter of course on his lips. Also, Bill Totts was a trifle inclined to late hours, and at times, in saloons, to be good-naturedly bellicose with other workmen. Then, too, at Sunday picnics or when coming home from the show, either arm betrayed a practised familiarity in stealing around girls' waists, while he displayed a wit keen and delightful in the flirtatious badinage that was expected of a good fellow in his class.

So thoroughly was Bill Totts himself, so thoroughly a workman, a genuine denizen of South of the Slot, that he was as class-conscious as the average of his kind, and his hatred for a scab even exceeded that of the average loyal union man. During the Water Front Strike, Freddie Drummond was somehow able to stand apart from the unique combination, and, coldly critical, watch Bill Totts hilariously slug scab longshoremen. For Bill Totts was a dues-paying member of the Longshoremen

Union and had a right to be indignant with the usurpers of his job. "Big" Bill Totts was so very big, and so very able, that it was "Big" Bill to the front when trouble was brewing. From acting outraged feelings, Freddie Drummond, in the rôle of his other self, came to experience genuine outrage, and it was only when he returned to the classic atmosphere of the university that he was able, sanely and conservatively, to generalize upon his underworld experiences and put them down on paper as a trained sociologist should. That Bill Totts lacked the perspective to raise him above class-consciousness Freddie Drummond clearly saw. But Bill Totts could not see it. When he saw a scab taking his job away, he saw red at the same time, and little else did he see. It was Freddie Drummond, irreproachably clothed and comported, seated at his study desk or facing his class in Sociology 17, who saw Bill Totts, and all around Bill Totts, and all around the whole scab and union-labour problem and its relation to the economic welfare of the United States in the struggle for the world market. Bill Totts really wasn't able to see beyond the next meal and the prize-fight the following night at the Gaiety Athletic Club.

It was while gathering material for Women and Work that Freddie received his first warning of the danger he was in. He was too successful at living in both worlds. This strange dualism he had developed was after all very unstable, and, as he sat in his study and meditated, he saw that it could not endure. It was really a transition stage, and if he persisted he saw that he would inevitably have to drop one world or the other. He could not continue in both. And as he looked at the row of volumes that graced the upper shelf of his revolving book-case, his volumes, beginning with his Thesis and ending with Women and Work, he decided that that was the world he would hold to and stick by. Bill Totts had served his purpose, but he had become a too dangerous accomplice. Bill Totts would have to cease.

Freddie Drummond's fright was due to Mary Condon, President of the International Glove Workers' Union No. 974. He had seen her, first, from the spectators' gallery, at the annual convention of the Northwest Federation of Labour, and he had seen her through Bill Totts' eyes, and that individual had been most favourably impressed by her. She was not Freddie Drummond's sort at all. What if she were a royal-bodied woman, graceful and sinewy as a panther, with amazing black eyes that could fill with fire or laughter-love, as the mood might dictate? He detested women with a too exuberant vitality and a lack of . . . well, of inhibition. Freddie Drummond accepted the doctrine of evolution because it was quite universally accepted by college men, and he flatly believed that man had climbed up the ladder of life out of the weltering muck and mess of lower and monstrous organic things. But he was a trifle ashamed of this genealogy, and preferred not to think of it. Wherefore, probably, he practised his iron inhibition and preached it to others, and preferred women of his own type, who could shake free of this bestial and regrettable ancestral line and by discipline and control emphasize the wideness of the gulf that separated them from what their dim forbears had been.

Bill Totts had none of these considerations. He had liked Mary Condon from the moment his eyes first rested on her in the convention hall, and he had made it a point, then and there, to find out who she was. The next time he met her, and quite by accident, was when he was driving an express waggon for Pat Morrissey. It was in a lodging-house in Mission Street, where he had been called to take a trunk into storage. The landlady's daughter had called him and led him to the little bedroom, the occupant of which, a glove-maker, had just been removed to hospital. But Bill did not know this. He stooped, up-ended the trunk, which was a large one, got it on his shoulder, and struggled to his feet with his back toward the open door. At that moment he heard a woman's voice.

"Belong to the union?" was the question asked.

"Aw, what's it to you?" he retorted. "Run along now, an' git outa my way. I wanta turn round."

The next he know, big as he was, he was whirled half around and sent reeling backward, the trunk overbalancing him, till he fetched up with a crash against the wall. He started to swear, but at the same instant found himself looking into Mary Condon's flashing, angry eyes.

"Of course I b'long to the union," he said. "I was only kiddin' you."

"Where's your card?" she demanded in businesslike tones.

"In my pocket. But I can't git it out now. This trunk's too damn heavy. Come on down to the waggon an' I'll show it to you."

"Put that trunk down," was the command.

"What for? I got a card, I'm tellin' you."

"Put it down, that's all. No scab's going to handle that trunk. You ought to be ashamed of yourself, you big coward, scabbing on honest men. Why don't you join the union and be a man?"

Mary Condon's colour had left her face, and it was apparent that she was in a rage.

"To think of a big man like you turning traitor to his class. I suppose you're aching to join the militia for a chance to shoot down union drivers the next strike. You may belong to the militia already, for that matter. You're the sort—"

"Hold on, now, that's too much!" Bill dropped the trunk to the floor with a bang, straightened up, and thrust his hand into his inside coat pocket. "I told you I was only kiddin'. There, look at that."

It was a union card properly enough.

"All right, take it along," Mary Condon said. "And the next time don't kid."

Her face relaxed as she noticed the ease with which he got the big trunk to his shoulder, and her eyes glowed as they glanced over the graceful massiveness of the man. But Bill did not see that. He was too busy with the trunk.

The next time he saw Mary Condon was during the Laundry Strike. The Laundry Workers, but recently organized, were green at the business, and had petitioned Mary Condon to engineer the strike. Freddie Drummond had had an inkling of what was coming, and had sent Bill Totts to join the union and investigate. Bill's job was in the wash-room, and the men had been called out first, that morning, in order to stiffen the courage of the girls; and Bill chanced to be near the door to the mangle-room when Mary Condon started to enter. The superintendent, who was both large and stout, barred her way. He wasn't going to have his girls called out, and he'd teach her a lesson to mind her own business. And as Mary tried to squeeze past him he thrust her back with a fat hand on her shoulder. She glanced around and saw Bill.

"Here you, Mr. Totts," she called. "Lend a hand. I want to get in."

Bill experienced a startle of warm surprise. She had remembered his name from his union card. The next moment the superintendent had been plucked from the doorway raving about rights under the law, and the girls were deserting their machines. During the rest of that short and successful strike,

Bill constituted himself Mary Condon's henchman and messenger, and when it was over returned to the University to be Freddie Drummond and to wonder what Bill Totts could see in such a woman.

Freddie Drummond was entirely safe, but Bill had fallen in love. There was no getting away from the fact of it, and it was this fact that had given Freddie Drummond his warning. Well, he had done his work, and his adventures could cease. There was no need for him to cross the Slot again. All but the last three chapters of his latest, Labour Tactics and Strategy, was finished, and he had sufficient material on hand adequately to supply those chapters.

Another conclusion he arrived at, was that in order to sheet-anchor himself as Freddie Drummond, closer ties and relations in his own social nook were necessary. It was time that he was married, anyway, and he was fully aware that if Freddie Drummond didn't get married, Bill Totts assuredly would, and the complications were too awful to contemplate. And so, enters Catherine Van Vorst. She was a college woman herself, and her father, the one wealthy member of the faculty, was the head of the Philosophy Department as well. It would be a wise marriage from every standpoint, Freddie Drummond concluded when the engagement was consummated and announced. In appearance cold and reserved, aristocratic and wholesomely conservative, Catherine Van Vorst, though warm in her way, possessed an inhibition equal to Drummond's.

All seemed well with him, but Freddie Drummond could not quite shake off the call of the underworld, the lure of the free and open, of the unhampered, irresponsible life South of the Slot. As the time of his marriage approached, he felt that he had indeed sowed wild oats, and he felt, moreover, what a good thing it would be if he could have but one wild fling more, play the good fellow and the wastrel one last time, ere he settled down to grey lecture-rooms and sober matrimony. And, further to tempt him, the very last chapter of Labour Tactics and Strategy remained unwritten for lack of a trifle more of essential data which he had neglected to gather.

So Freddie Drummond went down for the last time as Bill Totts, got his data, and, unfortunately, encountered Mary Condon. Once more installed in his study, it was not a pleasant thing to look back upon. It made his warning doubly imperative. Bill Totts had behaved abominably. Not only had he met Mary Condon at the Central Labour Council, but he had stopped at a chop-house with her, on the way home, and treated her to oysters. And before they parted at her door, his arms had been about her, and he had kissed her on the lips and kissed her repeatedly. And her last words in his ear, words uttered softly with a catchy sob in the throat that was nothing more nor less than a love cry, were "Bill . . . dear, dear Bill."

Freddie Drummond shuddered at the recollection. He saw the pit yawning for him. He was not by nature a polygamist, and he was appalled at the possibilities of the situation. It would have to be put an end to, and it would end in one only of two ways: either he must become wholly Bill Totts and be married to Mary Condon, or he must remain wholly Freddie Drummond and be married to Catherine Van Vorst. Otherwise, his conduct would be beneath contempt and horrible.

In the several months that followed, San Francisco was torn with labour strife. The unions and the employers' associations had locked horns with a determination that looked as if they intended to settle the matter, one way or the other, for all time. But Freddie Drummond corrected proofs, lectured classes, and did not budge. He devoted himself to Catherine Van Vorst, and day by day found more to respect and admire in her, nay, even to love in her. The Street Car Strike tempted him, but not so severely as he would have expected; and the great Meat Strike came on and left him cold. The ghost of Bill Totts had been successfully laid, and Freddie Drummond with rejuvenescent zeal tackled a brochure, long-planned, on the topic of "diminishing returns."

The wedding was two weeks off, when, one afternoon, in San Francisco, Catherine Van Vorst picked him up and whisked him away to see a Boys' Club, recently instituted by the settlement workers in whom she was interested. It was her brother's machine, but they were alone with the exception of the chauffeur. At the junction with Kearny Street, Market and Geary Streets intersect like the sides of a sharp-angled letter "V." They, in the auto, were coming down Market with the intention of negotiating the sharp apex and going up Geary. But they did not know what was coming down Geary, timed by fate to meet them at the apex. While aware from the papers that the Meat Strike was on and that it was an exceedingly bitter one, all thought of it at that moment was farthest from Freddie Drummond's mind. Was he not seated beside Catherine? And besides, he was carefully expositing to her his views on settlement work, views that Bill Totts' adventures had played a part in formulating.

Coming down Geary Street were six meat waggons. Beside each scab driver sat a policeman. Front and rear, and along each side of this procession, marched a protecting escort of one hundred police. Behind the police rearguard, at a respectful distance, was an orderly but vociferous mob, several blocks in length, that congested the street from sidewalk to sidewalk. The Beef Trust was making an effort to supply the hotels, and, incidentally, to begin the breaking of the strike. The St. Francis had already been supplied, at a cost of many broken windows and broken heads, and the expedition was marching to the relief of the Palace Hotel.

All unwitting, Drummond sat beside Catherine, talking settlement work, as the auto, honking methodically and dodging traffic, swung in a wide curve to get around the apex. A big coal waggon, loaded with lump coal and drawn by four huge horses, just debouching from Kearny Street as though to turn down Market, blocked their way. The driver of the waggon seemed undecided, and the chauffeur, running slow but disregarding some shouted warning from the crossing policemen, swerved the auto to the left, violating the traffic rules, in order to pass in front of the waggon.

At that moment Freddie Drummond discontinued his conversation. Nor did he resume it again, for the situation was developing with the rapidity of a transformation scene. He heard the roar of the mob at the rear, and caught a glimpse of the helmeted police and the lurching meat waggons. At the same moment, laying on his whip, and standing up to his task, the coal driver rushed horses and waggon squarely in front of the advancing procession, pulled the horses up sharply, and put on the big brake. Then he made his lines fast to the brake-handle and sat down with the air of one who had stopped to stay. The auto had been brought to a stop, too, by his big panting leaders which had jammed against it.

Before the chauffeur could back clear, an old Irishman, driving a rickety express waggon and lashing his one horse to a gallop, had locked wheels with the auto. Drummond recognized both horse and waggon, for he had driven them often himself. The Irishman was Pat Morrissey. On the other side a brewery waggon was locking with the coal waggon, and an east-bound Kearny Street car, wildly clanging its gong, the motorman shouting defiance at the crossing policeman, was dashing forward to complete the blockade. And waggon after waggon was locking and blocking and adding to the confusion. The meat waggons halted. The police were trapped. The roar at the rear increased as the mob came on to the attack, while the vanguard of the police charged the obstructing waggons.

"We're in for it," Drummond remarked coolly to Catherine.

"Yes," she nodded, with equal coolness. "What savages they are."

His admiration for her doubled on itself. She was indeed his sort. He would have been satisfied with her even if she had screamed, and clung to him, but this, this was magnificent. She sat in that storm centre as calmly as if it had been no more than a block of carriages at the opera.

The police were struggling to clear a passage. The driver of the coal waggon, a big man in shirt sleeves, lighted a pipe and sat smoking. He glanced down complacently at a captain of police who was raving and cursing at him, and his only acknowledgment was a shrug of the shoulders. From the rear arose the rat-rat-tat of clubs on heads and a pandemonium of cursing, yelling, and shouting. A violent accession of noise proclaimed that the mob had broken through and was dragging a scab from a waggon. The police captain reinforced from his vanguard, and the mob at the rear was repelled. Meanwhile, window after window in the high office building on the right had been opened, and the class-conscious clerks were raining a shower of office furniture down on the heads of police and scabs. Waste-baskets, ink-bottles, paper-weights, type-writers, anything and everything that came to hand was filling the air.

A policeman, under orders from his captain, clambered to the lofty seat of the coal waggon to arrest the driver. And the driver, rising leisurely and peacefully to meet him, suddenly crumpled him in his arms and threw him down on top of the captain. The driver was a young giant, and when he climbed on his load and poised a lump of coal in both hands, a policeman, who was just scaling the waggon from the side, let go and dropped back to earth. The captain ordered half-a-dozen of his men to take the waggon. The teamster, scrambling over the load from side to side, beat them down with huge lumps of coal.

The crowd on the sidewalks and the teamsters on the locked waggons roared encouragement and their own delight. The motorman, smashing helmets with his controller bar, was beaten into insensibility and dragged from his platform. The captain of police, beside himself at the repulse of his men, led the next assault on the coal waggon. A score of police were swarming up the tall-sided fortress. But the teamster multiplied himself. At times there were six or eight policemen rolling on the pavement and under the waggon. Engaged in repulsing an attack on the rear end of his fortress, the teamster turned about to see the captain just in the act of stepping on to the seat from the front end. He was still in the air and in most unstable equilibrium, when the teamster hurled a thirty-pound lump of coal. It caught the captain fairly on the chest, and he went over backward, striking on a wheeler's back, tumbling on to the ground, and jamming against the rear wheel of the auto.

Catherine thought he was dead, but he picked himself up and charged back. She reached out her gloved hand and patted the flank of the snorting, quivering horse. But Drummond did not notice the action. He had eyes for nothing save the battle of the coal waggon, while somewhere in his complicated psychology, one Bill Totts was heaving and straining in an effort to come to life. Drummond believed in law and order and the maintenance of the established, but this riotous savage within him would have none of it. Then, if ever, did Freddie Drummond call upon his iron inhibition to save him. But it is written that the house divided against itself must fall. And Freddie Drummond found that he had divided all the will and force of him with Bill Totts, and between them the entity that constituted the pair of them was being wrenched in twain.

Freddie Drummond sat in the auto, quite composed, alongside Catherine Van Vorst; but looking out of Freddie Drummond's eyes was Bill Totts, and somewhere behind those eyes, battling for the control of their mutual body, were Freddie Drummond the sane and conservative sociologist, and Bill Totts, the class-conscious and bellicose union working man. It was Bill Totts, looking out of those eyes, who saw the inevitable end of the battle on the coal waggon. He saw a policeman gain the top of the load, a second, and a third. They lurched clumsily on the loose footing, but their long riot-clubs were out and swinging. One blow caught the teamster on the head. A second he dodged, receiving it on the shoulder. For him the game was plainly up. He dashed in suddenly, clutched two policemen in his arms, and hurled himself a prisoner to the pavement, his hold never relaxing on his two captors.

Catherine Van Vorst was sick and faint at sight of the blood and brutal fighting. But her qualms were vanquished by the sensational and most unexpected happening that followed. The man beside her emitted an unearthly and uncultured yell and rose to his feet. She saw him spring over the front seat, leap to the broad rump of the wheeler, and from there gain the waggon. His onslaught was like a whirlwind. Before the bewildered officer on the load could guess the errand of this conventionally clad but excited-seeming gentleman, he was the recipient of a punch that arched him back through the air to the pavement. A kick in the face led an ascending policeman to follow his example. A rush of three more gained the top and locked with Bill Totts in a gigantic clinch, during which his scalp was opened up by a club, and coat, vest, and half his starched shirt were torn from him. But the three policemen were flung far and wide, and Bill Totts, raining down lumps of coal, held the fort.

The captain led gallantly to the attack, but was bowled over by a chunk of coal that burst on his head in black baptism. The need of the police was to break the blockade in front before the mob could break in at the rear, and Bill Totts' need was to hold the waggon till the mob did break through. So the battle of the coal went on.

The crowd had recognized its champion. "Big" Bill, as usual, had come to the front, and Catherine Van Vorst was bewildered by the cries of "Bill! O you Bill!" that arose on every hand. Pat Morrissey, on his waggon seat, was jumping and screaming in an ecstasy, "Eat 'em, Bill! Eat 'em! Eat 'em alive!" From the sidewalk she heard a woman's voice cry out, "Look out, Bill—front end!" Bill took the warning and with well-directed coal cleared the front end of the waggon of assailants. Catherine Van Vorst turned her head and saw on the curb of the sidewalk a woman with vivid colouring and flashing black eyes who was staring with all her soul at the man who had been Freddie Drummond a few minutes before.

The windows of the office building became vociferous with applause. A fresh shower of office chairs and filing cabinets descended. The mob had broken through on one side the line of waggons, and was advancing, each segregated policeman the centre of a fighting group. The scabs were torn from their seats, the traces of the horses cut, and the frightened animals put in flight. Many policemen crawled under the coal waggon for safety, while the loose horses, with here and there a policeman on their backs or struggling at their heads to hold them, surged across the sidewalk opposite the jam and broke into Market Street.

Catherine Van Vorst heard the woman's voice calling in warning. She was back on the curb again, and crying out—

"Beat it, Bill! Now's your time! Beat it!"

The police for the moment had been swept away. Bill Totts leaped to the pavement and made his way to the woman on the sidewalk. Catherine Van Vorst saw her throw her arms around him and kiss him on the lips; and Catherine Van Vorst watched him curiously as he went on down the sidewalk, one arm around the woman, both talking and laughing, and he with a volubility and abandon she could never have dreamed possible.

The police were back again and clearing the jam while waiting for reinforcements and new drivers and horses. The mob had done its work and was scattering, and Catherine Van Vorst, still watching, could see the man she had known as Freddie Drummond. He towered a head above the crowd. His arm was still about the woman. And she in the motor-car, watching, saw the pair cross Market Street, cross the Slot, and disappear down Third Street into the labour ghetto.

In the years that followed no more lectures were given in the University of California by one Freddie Drummond, and no more books on economics and the labour question appeared over the name of Frederick A. Drummond. On the other hand there arose a new labour leader, William Totts by name. He it was who married Mary Condon, President of the International Glove Workers' Union No. 974; and he it was who called the notorious Cooks and Waiters' Strike, which, before its successful termination, brought out with it scores of other unions, among which, of the more remotely allied, were the Chicken Pickers and the Undertakers.

THE UNPARALLELED INVASION

It was in the year 1976 that the trouble between the world and China reached its culmination. It was because of this that the celebration of the Second Centennial of American Liberty was deferred. Many other plans of the nations of the earth were twisted and tangled and postponed for the same reason. The world awoke rather abruptly to its danger; but for over seventy years, unperceived, affairs had been shaping toward this very end.

The year 1904 logically marks the beginning of the development that, seventy years later, was to bring consternation to the whole world. The Japanese-Russian War took place in 1904, and the historians of the time gravely noted it down that that event marked the entrance of Japan into the comity of nations. What it really did mark was the awakening of China. This awakening, long expected, had finally been given up. The Western nations had tried to arouse China, and they had failed. Out of their native optimism and race-egotism they had therefore concluded that the task was impossible, that China would never awaken.

What they had failed to take into account was this: that between them and China was no common psychological speech. Their thought-processes were radically dissimilar. There was no intimate vocabulary. The Western mind penetrated the Chinese mind but a short distance when it found itself in a fathomless maze. The Chinese mind penetrated the Western mind an equally short distance when it fetched up against a blank, incomprehensible wall. It was all a matter of language. There was no way to communicate Western ideas to the Chinese mind. China remained asleep. The material achievement and progress of the West was a closed book to her; nor could the West open the book. Back and deep down on the tie-ribs of consciousness, in the mind, say, of the English-speaking race, was a capacity to thrill to short, Saxon words; back and deep down on the tie-ribs of consciousness of the Chinese mind was a capacity to thrill to its own hieroglyphics; but the Chinese mind could not thrill to short, Saxon words; nor could the English-speaking mind thrill to hieroglyphics. The fabrics of their minds were woven from totally different stuffs. They were mental aliens. And so it was that Western material achievement and progress made no dent on the rounded sleep of China.

Came Japan and her victory over Russia in 1904. Now the Japanese race was the freak and paradox among Eastern peoples. In some strange way Japan was receptive to all the West had to offer. Japan swiftly assimilated the Western ideas, and digested them, and so capably applied them that she suddenly burst forth, full-panoplied, a world-power. There is no explaining this peculiar openness of Japan to the alien culture of the West. As well might be explained any biological sport in the animal kingdom.

Having decisively thrashed the great Russian Empire, Japan promptly set about dreaming a colossal dream of empire for herself. Korea she had made into a granary and a colony; treaty privileges and vulpine diplomacy gave her the monopoly of Manchuria. But Japan was not satisfied. She turned her eyes upon China. There lay a vast territory, and in that territory were the hugest deposits in the world of iron and coal, the backbone of industrial civilization. Given natural resources, the other great factor in industry is labour. In that territory was a population of 400,000,000 souls, one quarter of the then total population of the earth. Furthermore, the Chinese were excellent workers, while their fatalistic philosophy (or religion) and their stolid nervous organization constituted them splendid soldiers, if they were properly managed. Needless to say, Japan was prepared to furnish that management.

But best of all, from the standpoint of Japan, the Chinese was a kindred race. The baffling enigma of the Chinese character to the West was no baffling enigma to the Japanese. The Japanese understood as we could never school ourselves or hope to understand. Their mental processes were the same. The Japanese thought with the same thought-symbols as did the Chinese, and they thought in the same peculiar grooves. Into the Chinese mind the Japanese went on where we were balked by the obstacle of incomprehension. They took the turning which we could not perceive, twisted around the obstacle, and were out of sight in the ramifications of the Chinese mind where we could not follow. They were brothers. Long ago one had borrowed the other's written language, and, untold generations before that, they had diverged from the common Mongol stock. There had been changes, differentiations brought about by diverse conditions and infusions of other blood; but down at the bottom of their beings, twisted into the fibres of them, was a heritage in common, a sameness in kind that time had not obliterated.

And so Japan took upon herself the management of China. In the years immediately following the war with Russia, her agents swarmed over the Chinese Empire. A thousand miles beyond the last mission station toiled her engineers and spies, clad as coolies, under the guise of itinerant merchants or proselytizing Buddhist priests, noting down the horse-power of every waterfall, the likely sites for factories, the heights of mountains and passes, the strategic advantages and weaknesses, the wealth of the farming valleys, the number of bullocks in a district or the number of labourers that could be collected by forced levies. Never was there such a census, and it could have been taken by no other people than the dogged, patient, patriotic Japanese.

But in a short time secrecy was thrown to the winds. Japan's officers reorganized the Chinese army; her drill sergeants made the mediæval warriors over into twentieth century soldiers, accustomed to all the modern machinery of war and with a higher average of marksmanship than the soldiers of any Western nation. The engineers of Japan deepened and widened the intricate system of canals, built factories and foundries, netted the empire with telegraphs and telephones, and inaugurated the era of railroad-building. It was these same protagonists of machine-civilization that discovered the great oil deposits of Chunsan, the iron mountains of Whang-Sing, the copper ranges of Chinchi, and they sank the gas wells of Wow-Wee, that most marvellous reservoir of natural gas in all the world.

In China's councils of empire were the Japanese emissaries. In the ears of the statesmen whispered the Japanese statesmen. The political reconstruction of the Empire was due to them. They evicted the scholar class, which was violently reactionary, and put into office progressive officials. And in every town and city of the Empire newspapers were started. Of course, Japanese editors ran the policy of these papers, which policy they got direct from Tokio. It was these papers that educated and made progressive the great mass of the population.

China was at last awake. Where the West had failed, Japan succeeded. She had transmuted Western culture and achievement into terms that were intelligible to the Chinese understanding. Japan herself, when she so suddenly awakened, had astounded the world. But at the time she was only forty millions strong. China's awakening, with her four hundred millions and the scientific advance of the world, was frightfully astounding. She was the colossus of the nations, and swiftly her voice was heard in no uncertain tones in the affairs and councils of the nations. Japan egged her on, and the proud Western peoples listened with respectful ears.

China's swift and remarkable rise was due, perhaps more than to anything else, to the superlative quality of her labour. The Chinese was the perfect type of industry. He had always been that. For sheer ability to work no worker in the world could compare with him. Work was the breath of his nostrils. It was to him what wandering and fighting in far lands and spiritual adventure had been to other peoples. Liberty, to him, epitomized itself in access to the means of toil. To till the soil and labour interminably was all he asked of life and the powers that be. And the awakening of China had given its vast population not merely free and unlimited access to the means of toil, but access to the highest and most scientific machine-means of toil.

China rejuvenescent! It was but a step to China rampant. She discovered a new pride in herself and a will of her own. She began to chafe under the guidance of Japan, but she did not chafe long. On Japan's advice, in the beginning, she had expelled from the Empire all Western missionaries, engineers, drill sergeants, merchants, and teachers. She now began to expel the similar representatives of Japan. The latter's advisory statesmen were showered with honours and decorations, and sent home. The West had awakened Japan, and, as Japan had then requited the West, Japan was not requited by China. Japan was thanked for her kindly aid and flung out bag and baggage by her gigantic protégé. The Western nations chuckled. Japan's rainbow dream had gone glimmering. She grew angry. China laughed at her. The blood and the swords of the Samurai would out, and Japan rashly went to war. This occurred in 1922, and in seven bloody months Manchuria, Korea, and Formosa were taken away from her and she was hurled back, bankrupt, to stifle in her tiny, crowded islands. Exit Japan from the world drama. Thereafter she devoted herself to art, and her task became to please the world greatly with her creations of wonder and beauty.

Contrary to expectation, China did not prove warlike. She had no Napoleonic dream, and was content to devote herself to the arts of peace. After a time of disquiet, the idea was accepted that China was to be feared, not in war, but in commerce. It will be seen that the real danger was not apprehended. China went on consummating her machine-civilization. Instead of a large standing army, she developed an immensely larger and splendidly efficient militia. Her navy was so small that it was the laughing stock of the world; nor did she attempt to strengthen her navy. The treaty ports of the world were never entered by her visiting battleships.

The real danger lay in the fecundity of her loins, and it was in 1970 that the first cry of alarm was raised. For some time all territories adjacent to China had been grumbling at Chinese immigration; but now it suddenly came home to the world that China's population was 500,000,000. She had increased by a hundred millions since her awakening. Burchaldter called attention to the fact that there were more Chinese in existence than white-skinned people. He performed a simple sum in arithmetic. He added together the populations of the United States, Canada, New Zealand, Australia, South Africa, England, France, Germany, Italy, Austria, European Russia, and all Scandinavia. The result was 495,000,000. And the population of China overtopped this tremendous total by 5,000,000. Burchaldter's figures went round the world, and the world shivered.

For many centuries China's population had been constant. Her territory had been saturated with population; that is to say, her territory, with the primitive method of production, had supported the maximum limit of population. But when she awoke and inaugurated the machine-civilization, her productive power had been enormously increased. Thus, on the same territory, she was able to support a far larger population. At once the birth rate began to rise and the death rate to fall. Before, when population pressed against the means of subsistence, the excess population had been swept away by famine. But now, thanks to the machine-civilization, China's means of subsistence had been enormously extended, and there were no famines; her population followed on the heels of the increase in the means of subsistence.

During this time of transition and development of power, China had entertained no dreams of conquest. The Chinese was not an imperial race. It was industrious, thrifty, and peace-loving. War was looked upon as an unpleasant but necessary task that at times must be performed. And so, while the Western races had squabbled and fought, and world-adventured against one another, China had calmly gone on working at her machines and growing. Now she was spilling over the boundaries of her Empire, that was all, just spilling over into the adjacent territories with all the certainty and terrifying slow momentum of a glacier.

Following upon the alarm raised by Burchaldter's figures, in 1970 France made a long-threatened stand. French Indo-China had been overrun, filled up, by Chinese immigrants. France called a halt. The Chinese wave flowed on. France assembled a force of a hundred thousand on the boundary between her unfortunate colony and China, and China sent down an army of militia-soldiers a million strong. Behind came the wives and sons and daughters and relatives, with their personal household luggage, in a second army. The French force was brushed aside like a fly. The Chinese militia-soldiers, along with their families, over five millions all told, coolly took possession of French Indo-China and settled down to stay for a few thousand years.

Outraged France was in arms. She hurled fleet after fleet against the coast of China, and nearly bankrupted herself by the effort. China had no navy. She withdrew like a turtle into her shell. For a year the French fleets blockaded the coast and bombarded exposed towns and villages. China did not mind. She did not depend upon the rest of the world for anything. She calmly kept out of range of the French guns and went on working. France wept and wailed, wrung her impotent hands and appealed to the dumfounded nations. Then she landed a punitive expedition to march to Peking. It was two hundred and fifty thousand strong, and it was the flower of France. It landed without opposition and marched into the interior. And that was the last ever seen of it. The line of communication was snapped on the second day. Not a survivor came back to tell what had happened. It had been swallowed up in China's cavernous maw, that was all.

In the five years that followed, China's expansion, in all land directions, went on apace. Siam was made part of the Empire, and, in spite of all that England could do, Burma and the Malay Peninsula were overrun; while all along the long south boundary of Siberia, Russia was pressed severely by China's advancing hordes. The process was simple. First came the Chinese immigration (or, rather, it was already there, having come there slowly and insidiously during the previous years). Next came the clash of arms and the brushing away of all opposition by a monster army of militia-soldiers, followed by their families and household baggage. And finally came their settling down as colonists in the conquered territory. Never was there so strange and effective a method of world conquest.

Napal and Bhutan were overrun, and the whole northern boundary of India pressed against by this fearful tide of life. To the west, Bokhara, and, even to the south and west, Afghanistan, were swallowed up. Persia, Turkestan, and all Central Asia felt the pressure of the flood. It was at this time that Burchaldter revised his figures. He had been mistaken. China's population must be seven hundred millions, eight hundred millions, nobody knew how many millions, but at any rate it would soon be a billion. There were two Chinese for every white-skinned human in the world, Burchaldter announced, and the world trembled. China's increase must have begun immediately, in 1904. It was remembered that since that date there had not been a single famine. At 5,000,000 a year increase, her total increase in the intervening seventy years must be 350,000,000. But who was to know? It might be more. Who was to know anything of this strange new menace of the twentieth century, China, old China, rejuvenescent, fruitful, and militant!

The Convention of 1975 was called at Philadelphia. All the Western nations, and some few of the Eastern, were represented. Nothing was accomplished. There was talk of all countries putting bounties on children to increase the birth rate, but it was laughed to scorn by the arithmeticians, who pointed out that China was too far in the lead in that direction. No feasible way of coping with China was suggested. China was appealed to and threatened by the United Powers, and that was all the Convention of Philadelphia came to; and the Convention and the Powers were laughed at by China. Li Tang Fwung, the power behind the Dragon Throne, deigned to reply.

"What does China care for the comity of nations?" said Li Tang Fwung. "We are the most ancient, honourable, and royal of races. We have our own destiny to accomplish. It is unpleasant that our destiny does not tally with the destiny of the rest of the world, but what would you? You have talked windily about the royal races and the heritage of the earth, and we can only reply that that remains to be seen. You cannot invade us. Never mind about your navies. Don't shout. We know our navy is small. You see we use it for police purposes. We do not care for the sea. Our strength is in our population, which will soon be a billion. Thanks to you, we are equipped with all modern war-machinery. Send your navies. We will not notice them. Send your punitive expeditions, but first remember France. To land half a million soldiers on our shores would strain the resources of any of you. And our thousand millions would swallow them down in a mouthful. Send a million; send five millions, and we will swallow them down just as readily. Pouf! A mere nothing, a meagre morsel. Destroy, as you have threatened, you United States, the ten million coolies we have forced upon your shores, why, the amount scarcely equals half of our excess birth rate for a year."

So spoke Li Tang Fwung. The world was nonplussed, helpless, terrified. Truly had he spoken. There was no combating China's amazing birth rate. If her population was a billion, and was increasing twenty millions a year, in twenty-five years it would be a billion and a half, equal to the total population of the world in 1904. And nothing could be done. There was no way to dam up the over-spilling monstrous flood of life. War was futile. China laughed at a blockade of her coasts. She welcomed invasion. In her capacious maw was room for all the hosts of earth that could be hurled at her. And in the meantime her flood of yellow life poured out and on over Asia. China laughed and read in their magazines the learned lucubrations of the distracted Western scholars.

But there was one scholar China failed to reckon on, Jacobus Laningdale. Not that he was a scholar, except in the widest sense. Primarily, Jacobus Laningdale was a scientist, and, up to that time, a very obscure scientist, a professor employed in the laboratories of the Health Office of New York City. Jacobus Laningdale's head was very like any other head, but in that head was evolved an idea. Also, in that head was the wisdom to keep that idea secret. He did not write an article for the magazines. Instead, he asked for a vacation. On September 19, 1975, he arrived in Washington. It was evening, but he proceeded straight to the White House, for he had already arranged an audience with the President. He was closeted with President Moyer for three hours. What passed between them was not learned by the rest of the world until long after; in fact, at that time the world was not interested in Jacobus Laningdale. Next day the President called in his Cabinet. Jacobus Laningdale was present. The proceedings were kept secret. But that very afternoon Rufus Cowdery, Secretary of State, left Washington, and early the following morning sailed for England. The secret that he carried began to spread, but it spread only among the heads of Governments. Possibly half-a-dozen men in a nation were entrusted with the idea that had formed in Jacobus Laningdale's head.

Following the spread of the secret, sprang up great activity in all the dockyards, arsenals, and navy-yards. The people of France and Austria became suspicious, but so sincere were their Governments' calls for confidence that they acquiesced in the unknown project that was afoot.

This was the time of the Great Truce. All countries pledged themselves solemnly not to go to war with any other country. The first definite action was the gradual mobilization of the armies of Russia, Germany, Austria, Italy, Greece, and Turkey. Then began the eastward movement. All railroads into Asia were glutted with troop trains. China was the objective, that was all that was known. A little later began the great sea movement. Expeditions of warships were launched from all countries. Fleet followed fleet, and all proceeded to the coast of China. The nations cleaned out their navy-yards. They sent their revenue cutters and dispatch boots and lighthouse tenders, and they sent their last antiquated cruisers and battleships. Not content with this, they impressed the merchant marine. The statistics show that 58,640 merchant steamers, equipped with searchlights and rapid-fire guns, were despatched by the various nations to China.

And China smiled and waited. On her land side, along her boundaries, were millions of the warriors of Europe. She mobilized five times as many millions of her militia and awaited the invasion. On her sea coasts she did the same. But China was puzzled. After all this enormous preparation, there was no invasion. She could not understand. Along the great Siberian frontier all was quiet. Along her coasts the towns and villages were not even shelled. Never, in the history of the world, had there been so mighty a gathering of war fleets. The fleets of all the world were there, and day and night millions of tons of battleships ploughed the brine of her coasts, and nothing happened. Nothing was attempted. Did they think to make her emerge from her shell? China smiled. Did they think to tire her out, or starve her out? China smiled again.

But on May 1, 1976, had the reader been in the imperial city of Peking, with its then population of eleven millions, he would have witnessed a curious sight. He would have seen the streets filled with the chattering yellow populace, every queued head tilted back, every slant eye turned skyward. And high up in the blue he would have beheld a tiny dot of black, which, because of its orderly evolutions, he would have identified as an airship. From this airship, as it curved its flight back and forth over the city, fell missiles, strange, harmless missiles, tubes of fragile glass that shattered into thousands of fragments on the streets and house-tops. But there was nothing deadly about these tubes of glass. Nothing happened. There were no explosions. It is true, three Chinese were killed by the tubes dropping on their heads from so enormous a height; but what were three Chinese against an excess birth rate of twenty millions? One tube struck perpendicularly in a fish-pond in a garden and was not broken. It was dragged ashore by the master of the house. He did not dare to open it, but, accompanied by his friends, and surrounded by an ever-increasing crowd, he carried the mysterious tube to the magistrate of the district. The latter was a brave man. With all eyes upon him, he shattered the tube with a blow from his brass-bowled pipe. Nothing happened. Of those who were very near, one or two thought they saw some mosquitoes fly out. That was all. The crowd set up a great laugh and dispersed.

As Peking was bombarded by glass tubes, so was all China. The tiny airships, dispatched from the warships, contained but two men each, and over all cities, towns, and villages they wheeled and curved, one man directing the ship, the other man throwing over the glass tubes.

Had the reader again been in Peking, six weeks later, he would have looked in vain for the eleven million inhabitants. Some few of them he would have found, a few hundred thousand, perhaps, their carcasses festering in the houses and in the deserted streets, and piled high on the abandoned death-waggons. But for the rest he would have had to seek along the highways and byways of the Empire. And not all would he have found fleeing from plague-stricken Peking, for behind them, by hundreds of thousands of unburied corpses by the wayside, he could have marked their flight. And as it was with Peking, so it was with all the cities, towns, and villages of the Empire. The plague smote them all. Nor was it one plague, nor two plagues; it was a score of plagues. Every virulent form of infectious death stalked through the land. Too late the Chinese government apprehended the meaning of the colossal preparations, the marshalling of the world-hosts, the flights of the tin airships, and the rain of the tubes of glass. The proclamations of the government were vain. They could not stop the eleven million plague-stricken wretches, fleeing from the one city of Peking to spread disease through all the land. The physicians and health officers died at their posts; and death, the all-conqueror, rode over the decrees of the Emperor and Li Tang Fwung. It rode over them as well, for Li Tang Fwung died in the second week, and the Emperor, hidden away in the Summer Palace, died in the fourth week.

Had there been one plague, China might have coped with it. But from a score of plagues no creature was immune. The man who escaped smallpox went down before scarlet fever. The man who was immune to yellow fever was carried away by cholera; and if he were immune to that, too, the Black Death, which was the bubonic plague, swept him away. For it was these bacteria, and germs, and microbes, and bacilli, cultured in the laboratories of the West, that had come down upon China in the rain of glass.

All organization vanished. The government crumbled away. Decrees and proclamations were useless when the men who made them and signed them one moment were dead the next. Nor could the maddened millions, spurred on to flight by death, pause to heed anything. They fled from the cities to infect the country, and wherever they fled they carried the plagues with them. The hot summer was on—Jacobus Laningdale had selected the time shrewdly—and the plague festered everywhere. Much is conjectured of what occurred, and much has been learned from the stories of the few survivors. The wretched creatures stormed across the Empire in many-millioned flight. The vast armies China had collected on her frontiers melted away. The farms were ravaged for food, and no more crops were planted, while the crops already in were left unattended and never came to harvest. The most remarkable thing, perhaps, was the flights. Many millions engaged in them, charging to the bounds of the Empire to be met and turned back by the gigantic armies of the West. The slaughter of the mad hosts on the boundaries was stupendous. Time and again the guarding line was drawn back twenty or thirty miles to escape the contagion of the multitudinous dead.

Once the plague broke through and seized upon the German and Austrian soldiers who were guarding the borders of Turkestan. Preparations had been made for such a happening, and though sixty thousand soldiers of Europe were carried off, the international corps of physicians isolated the contagion and dammed it back. It was during this struggle that it was suggested that a new plague-germ had originated, that in some way or other a sort of hybridization between plague-germs had taken place, producing a new and frightfully virulent germ. First suspected by Vomberg, who became infected with it and died, it was later isolated and studied by Stevens, Hazenfelt, Norman, and Landers.

Such was the unparalleled invasion of China. For that billion of people there was no hope. Pent in their vast and festering charnel-house, all organization and cohesion lost, they could do naught but die. They could not escape. As they were flung back from their land frontiers, so were they flung back from the sea. Seventy-five thousand vessels patrolled the coasts. By day their smoking funnels dimmed the sea-rim, and by night their flashing searchlights ploughed the dark and harrowed it for the tiniest escaping junk. The attempts of the immense fleets of junks were pitiful. Not one ever got by the guarding sea-hounds. Modern war-machinery held back the disorganized mass of China, while the plagues did the work.

But old War was made a thing of laughter. Naught remained to him but patrol duty. China had laughed at war, and war she was getting, but it was ultra-modern war, twentieth century war, the war of the scientist and the laboratory, the war of Jacobus Laningdale. Hundred-ton guns were toys compared with the micro-organic projectiles hurled from the laboratories, the messengers of death, the destroying angels that stalked through the empire of a billion souls.

During all the summer and fall of 1976 China was an inferno. There was no eluding the microscopic projectiles that sought out the remotest hiding-places. The hundreds of millions of dead remained unburied and the germs multiplied themselves, and, toward the last, millions died daily of starvation. Besides, starvation weakened the victims and destroyed their natural defences against the plagues. Cannibalism, murder, and madness reigned. And so perished China.

Not until the following February, in the coldest weather, were the first expeditions made. These expeditions were small, composed of scientists and bodies of troops; but they entered China from every side. In spite of the most elaborate precautions against infection, numbers of soldiers and a few of the physicians were stricken. But the exploration went bravely on. They found China devastated, a howling wilderness through which wandered bands of wild dogs and desperate bandits who had survived. All survivors were put to death wherever found. And then began the great task, the sanitation of China. Five years and hundreds of millions of treasure were consumed, and then the world moved in—not in zones, as was the idea of Baron Albrecht, but heterogeneously, according to the democratic American programme. It was a vast and happy intermingling of nationalities that settled down in China in 1982 and the years that followed—a tremendous and successful experiment in cross-fertilization. We know to-day the splendid mechanical, intellectual, and art output that followed.

It was in 1987, the Great Truce having been dissolved, that the ancient quarrel between France and Germany over Alsace-Lorraine recrudesced. The war-cloud grew dark and threatening in April, and on April 17 the Convention of Copenhagen was called. The representatives of the nations of the world, being present, all nations solemnly pledged themselves never to use against one another the laboratory methods of warfare they had employed in the invasion of China.

—Excerpt from Walt Mervin's "Certain Essays in History."

THE ENEMY OF ALL THE WORLD

IT was Silas Bannerman who finally ran down that scientific wizard and arch-enemy of mankind, Emil Gluck. Gluck's confession, before he went to the electric chair, threw much light upon the series of mysterious events, many apparently unrelated, that so perturbed the world between the years 1933 and 1941. It was not until that remarkable document was made public that the world dreamed of there being any connection between the assassination of the King and Queen of Portugal and the murders of the New York City police officers. While the deeds of Emil Gluck were all that was abominable, we cannot but feel, to a certain extent, pity for the unfortunate, malformed, and maltreated genius. This side of his story has never been told before, and from his confession and from the great mass of evidence and the documents and records of the time we are able to construct a fairly accurate portrait of him, and to discern the factors and pressures that moulded him into the human monster he became and that drove him onward and downward along the fearful path he trod.

Emil Gluck was born in Syracuse, New York, in 1895. His father, Josephus Gluck, was a special policeman and night watchman, who, in the year 1900, died suddenly of pneumonia. The mother, a pretty, fragile creature, who, before her marriage, had been a milliner, grieved herself to death over the loss of her husband. This sensitiveness of the mother was the heritage that in the boy became morbid and horrible.

In 1901, the boy, Emil, then six years of age, went to live with his aunt, Mrs. Ann Bartell. She was his mother's sister, but in her breast was no kindly feeling for the sensitive, shrinking boy. Ann Bartell was a vain, shallow, and heartless woman. Also, she was cursed with poverty and burdened with a husband who was a lazy, erratic ne'er-do-well. Young Emil Gluck was not wanted, and Ann Bartell could be trusted to impress this fact sufficiently upon him. As an illustration of the treatment he received in that early, formative period, the following instance is given.

When he had been living in the Bartell home a little more than a year, he broke his leg. He sustained the injury through playing on the forbidden roof, as all boys have done and will continue to do to the end of time. The leg was broken in two places between the knee and thigh. Emil, helped by his frightened playmates, managed to drag himself to the front sidewalk, where he fainted. The children of the neighbourhood were afraid of the hard-featured shrew who presided over the Bartell house; but, summoning their resolution, they rang the bell and told Ann Bartell of the accident. She did not even look at the little lad who lay stricken on the sidewalk, but slammed the door and went back to her wash-tub. The time passed. A drizzle came on, and Emil Gluck, out of his faint, lay sobbing in the rain. The leg should have been set immediately. As it was, the inflammation rose rapidly and made a nasty case of it. At the end of two hours, the indignant women of the neighbourhood protested to Ann Bartell. This time she came out and looked at the lad. Also she kicked him in the side as he lay helpless at her feet, and she hysterically disowned him. He was not her child, she said, and recommended that the ambulance be called to take him to the city receiving hospital. Then she went back into the house.

It was a woman, Elizabeth Shepstone, who came along, learned the situation, and had the boy placed on a shutter. It was she who called the doctor, and who, brushing aside Ann Bartell, had the boy carried into the house. When the doctor arrived, Ann Bartell promptly warned him that she would not pay him for his services. For two months the little Emil lay in bed, the first month on his back without once being turned over; and he lay neglected and alone, save for the occasional visits of the unremunerated and over-worked physician. He had no toys, nothing with which to beguile the long and tedious hours. No kind word was spoken to him, no soothing hand laid upon his brow, no single touch or act of loving tenderness, naught but the reproaches and harshness of Ann Bartell, and the continually reiterated information that he was not wanted. And it can well be understood, in such environment, how there was generated in the lonely, neglected boy much of the bitterness and hostility for his kind that later was to express itself in deeds so frightful as to terrify the world.

It would seem strange that, from the hands of Ann Bartell, Emil Gluck should have received a college education; but the explanation is simple. Her ne'er-do-well husband, deserting her, made a strike in the Nevada goldfields, and returned to her a many-times millionaire. Ann Bartell hated the boy, and immediately she sent him to the Farristown Academy, a hundred miles away. Shy and sensitive, a lonely and misunderstood little soul, he was more lonely than ever at Farristown. He never came home, at vacation, and holidays, as the other boys did. Instead, he wandered about the deserted buildings and grounds, befriended and misunderstood by the servants and gardeners, reading much, it is remembered, spending his days in the fields or before the fire-place with his nose poked always in the pages of some book. It was at this time that he over-used his eyes and was compelled to take up the wearing of glasses, which same were so prominent in the photographs of him published in the newspapers in 1941.

He was a remarkable student. Application such as his would have taken him far; but he did not need application. A glance at a text meant mastery for him. The result was that he did an immense amount of collateral reading and acquired more in half a year than did the average student in half-a-dozen years. In 1909, barely fourteen years of age, he was ready—"more than ready" the headmaster of the academy said, to enter Yale or Harvard. His juvenility prevented him from entering those universities, and so, in 1909, we find him a freshman at historic Bowdoin College. In 1913 he graduated with highest honours, and immediately afterward followed Professor Bradlough to Berkeley, California. The one friend that Emil Gluck discovered in all his life was Professor Bradlough. The latter's weak lungs had led him to exchange Maine for California, the removal being facilitated by the offer of a professorship in the State University. Throughout the year 1914, Emil Gluck resided in Berkeley and took special scientific courses. Toward the end of that year two deaths changed his prospects and his relations with life. The death of Professor Bradlough took from him the one friend he was ever to know, and the death of Ann Bartell left him penniless. Hating the unfortunate lad to the last, she cut him off with one hundred dollars.

The following year, at twenty years of age, Emil Gluck was enrolled as an instructor of chemistry in the University of California. Here the years passed quietly; he faithfully performed the drudgery that brought him his salary, and, a student always, he took half-a-dozen degrees. He was, among other things, a Doctor of Sociology, of Philosophy, and of Science, though he was known to the world, in later days, only as Professor Gluck.

He was twenty-seven years old when he first sprang into prominence in the newspapers through the publication of his book, Sex and Progress. The book remains to-day a milestone in the history and philosophy of marriage. It is a heavy tome of over seven hundred pages, painfully careful and accurate, and startlingly original. It was a book for scientists, and not one calculated to make a stir. But Gluck, in the last chapter, using barely three lines for it, mentioned the hypothetical desirability of trial marriages. At once the newspapers seized these three lines, "played them up yellow," as the slang was in those days, and set the whole world laughing at Emil Gluck, the bespectacled young professor of twenty-seven. Photographers snapped him, he was besieged by reporters, women's clubs throughout the land passed resolutions condemning him and his immoral theories; and on the floor of the California Assembly, while discussing the state appropriation to the University, a motion demanding the expulsion of Gluck was made under threat of withholding the appropriation, of course, none of his persecutors had read the book; the twisted newspaper version of only three lines of it was enough for them. Here began Emil Gluck's hatred for newspaper men. By them his serious and intrinsically valuable work of six years had been made a laughing-stock and a notoriety. To his dying day, and to their everlasting regret, he never forgave them.

It was the newspapers that were responsible for the next disaster that befell him. For the five years following the publication of his book he had remained silent, and silence for a lonely man is not good. One can conjecture sympathetically the awful solitude of Emil Gluck in that populous University; for he was without friends and without sympathy. His only recourse was books, and he went on reading and studying enormously. But in 1927 he accepted an invitation to appear before the Human Interest Society of Emeryville. He did not trust himself to speak, and as we write we have before us a copy of his learned paper. It is sober, scholarly, and scientific, and, it must also be added, conservative. But in one place he dealt with, and I quote his words, "the industrial and social revolution that is taking place in society." A reporter present seized upon the word "revolution," divorced it from the text, and wrote a garbled account that made Emil Gluck appear an anarchist. At once, "Professor Gluck, anarchist," flamed over the wires and was appropriately "featured" in all the newspapers in the land.

He had attempted to reply to the previous newspaper attack, but now he remained silent. Bitterness had already corroded his soul. The University faculty appealed to him to defend himself, but he sullenly declined, even refusing to enter in defence a copy of his paper to save himself from expulsion. He refused to resign, and was discharged from the University faculty. It must be added that political pressure had been put upon the University Regents and the President.

Persecuted, maligned, and misunderstood, the forlorn and lonely man made no attempt at retaliation. All his life he had been sinned against, and all his life he had sinned against no one. But his cup of bitterness was not yet full to overflowing. Having lost his position, and being without any income, he had to find work. His first place was at the Union Iron Works, in San Francisco, where he proved a most able draughtsman. It was here that he obtained his firsthand knowledge of battleships and their construction. But the reporters discovered him and featured him in his new vocation. He immediately resigned and found another place; but after the reporters had driven him away from half-a-dozen positions, he steeled himself to brazen out the newspaper persecution. This occurred when he started his electroplating establishment, in Oakland, on Telegraph Avenue. It was a small shop, employing three men and two boys. Gluck himself worked long hours. Night after night, as Policeman Carew testified on the stand, he did not leave the shop till one and two in the morning. It was during this period that he perfected the improved ignition device for gas-engines, the royalties from which ultimately made him wealthy.

He started his electroplating establishment early in the spring of 1928, and it was in the same year that he formed the disastrous love attachment for Irene Tackley. Now it is not to be imagined that an extraordinary creature such as Emil Gluck could be any other than an extraordinary lover. In addition to his genius, his loneliness, and his morbidness, it must be taken into consideration that he knew nothing about women. Whatever tides of desire flooded his being, he was unschooled in the conventional expression of them; while his excessive timidity was bound to make his love-making unusual. Irene Tackley was a rather pretty young woman, but shallow and light-headed. At the time she worked in a small candy store across the street from Gluck's shop. He used to come in and drink ice-cream sodas and lemon-squashes, and stare at her. It seems the girl did not care for him, and merely played with him. He was "queer," she said; and at another time she called him a crank when describing how he sat at the counter and peered at her through his spectacles, blushing and stammering when she took notice of him, and often leaving the shop in precipitate confusion.

Gluck made her the most amazing presents, a silver tea-service, a diamond ring, a set of furs, opera-glasses, a ponderous History of the World in many volumes, and a motor-cycle all silver-plated in his own shop. Enters now the girl's lover, putting his foot down, showing great anger, compelling her to return Gluck's strange assortment of presents. This man, William Sherbourne, was a gross and stolid creature, a heavy-jawed man of the working class who had become a successful building-contractor in a small way. Gluck did not understand. He tried to get an explanation, attempting to speak with the girl when she went home from work in the evening. She complained to Sherbourne, and one night he gave Gluck a beating. It was a very severe beating, for it is on the records of the Red Cross Emergency Hospital that Gluck was treated there that night and was unable to leave the hospital for a week.

Still Gluck did not understand. He continued to seek an explanation from the girl. In fear of Sherbourne, he applied to the Chief of Police for permission to carry a revolver, which permission was refused, the newspapers as usual playing it up sensationally. Then came the murder of Irene Tackley, six days before her contemplated marriage with Sherbourne. It was on a Saturday night. She had worked late in the candy store, departing after eleven o'clock with her week's wages in her purse. She rode on a San Pablo Avenue surface car to Thirty-fourth Street, where she alighted and started to walk the three blocks to her home. That was the last seen of her alive. Next morning she was found, strangled, in a vacant lot.

Emil Gluck was immediately arrested. Nothing that he could do could save him. He was convicted, not merely on circumstantial evidence, but on evidence "cooked up" by the Oakland police. There is no discussion but that a large portion of the evidence was manufactured. The testimony of Captain Shehan was the sheerest perjury, it being proved long afterward that on the night in question he had not only not been in the vicinity of the murder, but that he had been out of the city in a resort on the San Leandro Road. The unfortunate Gluck received life imprisonment in San Quentin, while the newspapers and the public held that it was a miscarriage of justice, that the death penalty should have been visited upon him.

Gluck entered San Quentin prison on April 17, 1929. He was then thirty-four years of age. And for three years and a half, much of the time in solitary confinement, he was left to meditate upon the injustice of man. It was during that period that his bitterness corroded home and he became a hater of all his kind. Three other things he did during the same period: he wrote his famous treatise, Human Morals, his remarkable brochure, The Criminal Sane, and he worked out his awful and monstrous scheme of revenge. It was an episode that had occurred in his electroplating establishment that suggested to him his unique weapon of revenge. As stated in his confession, he worked every detail out theoretically during his imprisonment, and was able, on his release, immediately to embark on his career of vengeance.

His release was sensational. Also it was miserably and criminally delayed by the soulless legal red tape then in vogue. On the night of February 1, 1932, Tim Haswell, a hold-up man, was shot during an attempted robbery by a citizen of Piedmont Heights. Tim Haswell lingered three days, during which time he not only confessed to the murder of Irene Tackley, but furnished conclusive proofs of the same. Bert Danniker, a convict dying of consumption in Folsom Prison, was implicated as accessory, and his confession followed. It is inconceivable to us of to-day, the bungling, dilatory processes of justice a generation ago. Emil Gluck was proved in February to be an innocent man, yet he was not released until the following October. For eight months, a greatly wronged man, he was compelled to undergo his unmerited punishment. This was not conducive to sweetness and light, and we can well imagine how he ate his soul with bitterness during those dreary eight months.

He came back to the world in the fall of 1932, as usual a "feature" topic in all the newspapers. The papers, instead of expressing heartfelt regret, continued their old sensational persecution. One paper did more, the San Francisco Intelligencer. John Hartwell, its editor, elaborated an ingenious theory that got around the confessions of the two criminals and went to show that Gluck was responsible, after all, for the murder of Irene Tackley. Hartwell died. And Sherbourne died too, while Policeman Phillipps was shot in the leg and discharged from the Oakland police force.

The murder of Hartwell was long a mystery. He was alone in his editorial office at the time. The reports of the revolver were heard by the office boy, who rushed in to find Hartwell expiring in his chair. What puzzled the police was the fact, not merely that he had been shot with his own revolver, but that the revolver had been exploded in the drawer of his desk. The bullets had torn through the front of the drawer and entered his body. The police scouted the theory of suicide, murder was dismissed as absurd, and the blame was thrown upon the Eureka Smokeless Cartridge Company. Spontaneous explosion was the police explanation, and the chemists of the cartridge company were well bullied at the inquest. But what the police did not know was that across the street, in the Mercer Building, Room 633, rented by Emil Gluck, had been occupied by Emil Gluck at the very moment Hartwell's revolver so mysteriously exploded.

At the time, no connection was made between Hartwell's death and the death of William Sherbourne. Sherbourne had continued to live in the home he had built for Irene Tackley, and one morning in January, 1933, he was found dead. Suicide was the verdict of the coroner's inquest, for he had been shot by his own revolver. The curious thing that happened that night was the shooting of Policeman Phillipps on the sidewalk in front of Sherbourne's house. The policeman crawled to a police telephone on the corner and rang up for an ambulance. He claimed that some one had shot him from behind in the leg. The leg in question was so badly shattered by three '38 calibre bullets that amputation was necessary. But when the police discovered that the damage had been done by his own revolver, a great laugh went up, and he was charged with having been drunk. In spite of his denial of having touched a drop, and of his persistent assertion that the revolver had been in his hip pocket and that he had not laid a finger to it, he was discharged from the force. Emil Gluck's confession, six years later, cleared the unfortunate policeman of disgrace, and he is alive to-day and in good health, the recipient of a handsome pension from the city.

Emil Gluck, having disposed of his immediate enemies, now sought a wider field, though his enmity for newspaper men and for the police remained always active. The royalties on his ignition device for gasolene-engines had mounted up while he lay in prison, and year by year the earning power of his invention increased. He was independent, able to travel wherever he willed over the earth and to glut his monstrous appetite for revenge. He had become a monomaniac and an anarchist, not a philosophic anarchist, merely, but a violent anarchist. Perhaps the word is misused, and he is better described as a nihilist, or an annihilist. It is known that he affiliated with none of the groups of terrorists. He operated wholly alone, but he created a thousandfold more terror and achieved a thousandfold more destruction than all the terrorist groups added together.

He signalized his departure from California by blowing up Fort Mason. In his confession he spoke of it as a little experiment, he was merely trying his hand. For eight years he wandered over the earth, a mysterious terror, destroying property to the tune of hundreds of millions of dollars, and destroying countless lives. One good result of his awful deeds was the destruction he wrought among the terrorists themselves. Every time he did anything the terrorists in the vicinity were gathered in by the police dragnet, and many of them were executed. Seventeen were executed at Rome alone, following the assassination of the Italian King.

Perhaps the most world-amazing achievement of his was the assassination of the King and Queen of Portugal. It was their wedding day. All possible precautions had been taken against the terrorists, and the way from the cathedral, through Lisbon's streets, was double-banked with troops, while a squad of two hundred mounted troopers surrounded the carriage. Suddenly the amazing thing happened. The automatic rifles of the troopers began to go off, as well as the rifles, in the immediate vicinity, of the double-banked infantry. In the excitement the muzzles of the exploding rifles were turned in all directions. The slaughter was terrible, horses, troops, spectators, and the King and Queen, were riddled with bullets. To complicate the affair, in different parts of the crowd behind the foot-soldiers, two terrorists had bombs explode on their persons. These bombs they had intended to throw if they got the opportunity. But who was to know this? The frightful havoc wrought by the bursting bombs but added to the confusion; it was considered part of the general attack.

One puzzling thing that could not be explained away was the conduct of the troopers with their exploding rifles. It seemed impossible that they should be in the plot, yet there were the hundreds their flying bullets had slain, including the King and Queen. On the other hand, more baffling than ever was the fact that seventy per cent. of the troopers themselves had been killed or wounded. Some explained this on the ground that the loyal foot-soldiers, witnessing the attack on the royal carriage, had opened fire on the traitors. Yet not one bit of evidence to verify this could be drawn from the survivors, though many were put to the torture. They contended stubbornly that they had not discharged their rifles at all, but that their rifles had discharged themselves. They were laughed at by the chemists, who held that, while it was just barely probable that a single cartridge, charged with the new smokeless powder, might spontaneously explode, it was beyond all probability and possibility for all the cartridges in a given area, so charged, spontaneously to explode. And so, in the end, no explanation of the amazing occurrence was reached. The general opinion of the rest of the world was that the whole affair was a blind panic of the feverish Latins, precipitated, it was true, by the bursting of two terrorist bombs; and in this connection was recalled the laughable encounter of long years before between the Russian fleet and the English fishing boats.

And Emil Gluck chuckled and went his way. He knew. But how was the world to know? He had stumbled upon the secret in his old electroplating shop on Telegraph Avenue in the city of Oakland. It happened, at that time, that a wireless telegraph station was established by the Thurston Power Company close to his shop. In a short time his electroplating vat was put out of order. The vat-wiring had many bad joints, and, on investigation, Gluck discovered minute welds at the joints in the wiring. These, by lowering the resistance, had caused an excessive current to pass through the solution, "boiling" it and spoiling the work. But what had caused the welds? was the question in Gluck's mind. His reasoning was simple. Before the establishment of the wireless station, the vat had worked well. Not until after the establishment of the wireless station had the vat been ruined. Therefore the wireless station had been the cause. But how? He quickly answered the question. If an electric discharge was capable of operating a coherer across three thousand miles of ocean, then, certainly, the electric discharges from the wireless station four hundred feet away could produce coherer effects on the bad joints in the vat-wiring.

Gluck thought no more about it at the time. He merely re-wired his vat and went on electroplating. But afterwards, in prison, he remembered the incident, and like a flash there came into his mind the full significance of it. He saw in it the silent, secret weapon with which to revenge himself on the world. His great discovery, which died with him, was control over the direction and scope of the electric discharge. At the time, this was the unsolved problem of wireless telegraphy, as it still is to-day, but Emil Gluck, in his prison cell, mastered it. And, when he was released, he applied it. It was fairly simple, given the directing power that was his, to introduce a spark into the powder-magazines of a fort, a battleship, or a revolver. And not alone could he thus explode powder at a distance, but he could ignite conflagrations. The great Boston fire was started by him, quite by accident, however, as he stated in his confession, adding that it was a pleasing accident and that he had never had any reason to regret it.

It was Emil Gluck that caused the terrible German-American War, with the loss of 800,000 lives and the consumption of almost incalculable treasure. It will be remembered that in 1939, because of the Pickard incident, strained relations existed between the two countries. Germany, though aggrieved, was not anxious for war, and, as a peace token, sent the Crown Prince and seven battleships on a friendly visit to the United States. On the night of February 15, the seven warships lay at anchor in the Hudson opposite New York City. And on that night Emil Gluck, alone, with all his apparatus on board, was out in a launch. This launch, it was afterwards proved, was bought by him from the Ross Turner Company, while much of the apparatus he used that night had been purchased from the Columbia Electric Works. But this was not known at the time. All that was known was that the seven battleships blew up, one after another, at regular four-minute intervals. Ninety per cent. of the crews and officers, along with the Crown Prince, perished. Many years before, the American battleship Maine had been blown up in the harbour of Havana, and war with Spain had immediately followed, though there has always existed a reasonable doubt as to whether the explosion was due to conspiracy or accident. But accident could not explain the blowing up of the seven battleships on the Hudson at four-minute intervals. Germany believed that it had been done by a submarine, and immediately declared war. It was six months after Gluck's confession that she returned the Philippines and Hawaii to the United States.

In the meanwhile Emil Gluck, the malevolent wizard and arch-hater, travelled his whirlwind path of destruction. He left no traces. Scientifically thorough, he always cleaned up after himself. His method was to rent a room or a house, and secretly to install his apparatus, which apparatus, by the way, he so perfected and simplified that it occupied little space. After he had accomplished his purpose he carefully removed the apparatus. He bade fair to live out a long life of horrible crime.

The epidemic of shooting of New York City policemen was a remarkable affair. It became one of the horror mysteries of the time. In two short weeks over a hundred policemen were shot in the legs by their own revolvers. Inspector Jones did not solve the mystery, but it was his idea that finally outwitted Gluck. On his recommendation the policemen ceased carrying revolvers, and no more accidental shootings occurred.

It was in the early spring of 1940 that Gluck destroyed the Mare Island navy-yard. From a room in Vallejo he sent his electric discharges across the Vallejo Straits to Mare Island. He first played his flashes on the battleship Maryland. She lay at the dock of one of the mine-magazines. On her forward deck, on a huge temporary platform of timbers, were disposed over a hundred mines. These mines were for the defence of the Golden Gate. Any one of these mines was capable of destroying a dozen battleships, and there were over a hundred mines. The destruction was terrific, but it was only Gluck's overture. He played his flashes down the Mare Island shore, blowing up five torpedo boats, the torpedo station, and the great magazine at the eastern end of the island. Returning westward again, and scooping in occasional isolated magazines on the high ground back from the shore, he blew up three cruisers and the battleships Oregon, Delaware, New Hampshire, and Florida, the latter had just gone into dry-dock, and the magnificent dry-dock was destroyed along with her.

It was a frightful catastrophe, and a shiver of horror passed through the land. But it was nothing to what was to follow. In the late fall of that year Emil Gluck made a clean sweep of the Atlantic seaboard from Maine to Florida. Nothing escaped. Forts, mines, coast defences of all sorts, torpedo stations, magazines, everything went up. Three months afterward, in midwinter, he smote the north shore of the Mediterranean from Gibraltar to Greece in the same stupefying manner. A wail went up from the nations. It was clear that human agency was behind all this destruction, and it was equally clear, through Emil Gluck's impartiality, that the destruction was not the work of any particular nation. One thing was patent, namely, that whoever was the human behind it all, that human was a menace to the world. No nation was safe. There was no defence against this unknown and all-powerful foe. Warfare was futile, nay, not merely futile but itself the very essence of the peril. For a twelve-month the manufacture of powder ceased, and all soldiers and sailors were withdrawn from all fortifications and war vessels. And even a world-disarmament was seriously considered at the Convention of the Powers, held at The Hague at that time.

And then Silas Bannerman, a secret service agent of the United States, leaped into world-fame by arresting Emil Gluck. At first Bannerman was laughed at, but he had prepared his case well, and in a few weeks the most sceptical were convinced of Emil Gluck's guilt. The one thing, however, that Silas Bannerman never succeeded in explaining, even to his own satisfaction, was how first he came to connect Gluck with the atrocious crimes. It is true, Bannerman was in Vallejo, on secret government business, at the time of the destruction of Mare Island; and it is true that on the streets of Vallejo Emil Gluck was pointed out to him as a queer crank; but no impression was made at the time. It was not until afterward, when on a vacation in the Rocky Mountains and when reading the first published reports of the destruction along the Atlantic Coast, that suddenly Bannerman thought of Emil Gluck. And on the instant there flashed into his mind the connection between Gluck and the destruction. It was only an hypothesis, but it was sufficient. The great thing was the conception of the hypothesis, in itself an act of unconscious cerebration, a thing as unaccountable as the flashing, for instance, into Newton's mind of the principle of gravitation.

The rest was easy. Where was Gluck at the time of the destruction along the Atlantic sea-board? was the question that formed in Bannerman's mind. By his own request he was put upon the case. In no time he ascertained that Gluck had himself been up and down the Atlantic Coast in the late fall of 1940. Also he ascertained that Gluck had been in New York City during the epidemic of the shooting of police officers. Where was Gluck now? was Bannerman's next query. And, as if in answer, came the wholesale destruction along the Mediterranean. Gluck had sailed for Europe a month before, Bannerman knew that. It was not necessary for Bannerman to go to Europe. By means of cable messages and the co-operation of the European secret services, he traced Gluck's course along the Mediterranean and found that in every instance it coincided with the blowing up of coast defences and ships. Also, he learned that Gluck had just sailed on the Green Star liner Plutonic for the United States.

The case was complete in Bannerman's mind, though in the interval of waiting he worked up the details. In this he was ably assisted by George Brown, an operator employed by the Wood's System of Wireless Telegraphy. When the Plutonic arrived off Sandy Hook she was boarded by Bannerman from a Government tug, and Emil Gluck was made a prisoner. The trial and the confession followed. In the confession Gluck professed regret only for one thing, namely, that he had taken his time. As he said, had he dreamed that he was ever to be discovered he would have worked more rapidly and accomplished a thousand times the destruction he did. His secret died with him, though it is now known that the French Government managed to get access to him and offered him a billion francs for his invention wherewith he was able to direct and closely to confine electric discharges. "What!" was Gluck's reply, "to sell to you that which would enable you to enslave and maltreat suffering Humanity?" And though the war departments of the nations have continued to experiment in their secret laboratories, they have so far failed to light upon the slightest trace of the secret. Emil Gluck was executed on December 4, 1941, and so died, at the age of forty-six, one of the world's most unfortunate geniuses, a man of tremendous intellect, but whose mighty powers, instead of making toward good, were so twisted and warped that he became the most amazing of criminals.

—Culled from Mr. A. G. Burnside's "Eccentricitics of Crime," by kind permission of the publishers, Messrs. Holiday and Whitsund.

THE DREAM OF DEBS

I awoke fully an hour before my customary time. This in itself was remarkable, and I lay very wide awake, pondering over it. Something was the matter, something was wrong, I knew not what. I was oppressed by a premonition of something terrible that had happened or was about to happen. But what was it? I strove to orient myself. I remembered that at the time of the Great Earthquake of 1906 many claimed they awakened some moments before the first shock and that during these moments they experienced strange feelings of dread. Was San Francisco again to be visited by earthquake?

I lay for a full minute, numbly expectant, but there occurred no reeling of walls nor shock and grind of falling masonry. All was quiet. That was it! The silence! No wonder I had been perturbed. The hum of the great live city was strangely absent. The surface cars passed along my street, at that time of day, on an average of one every three minutes; but in the ten succeeding minutes not a car passed. Perhaps it was a street-railway strike, was my thought; or perhaps there had been an accident and the power was shut off. But no, the silence was too profound. I heard no jar and rattle of waggon wheels, nor stamp of iron-shod hoofs straining up the steep cobble-stones.

Pressing the push-button beside my bed, I strove to hear the sound of the bell, though I well knew it was impossible for the sound to rise three stories to me even if the bell did ring. It rang all right, for a few minutes later Brown entered with the tray and morning paper. Though his features were impassive as ever, I noted a startled, apprehensive light in his eyes. I noted, also, that there was no cream on the tray.

"The Creamery did not deliver this morning," he explained; "nor did the bakery."

I glanced again at the tray. There were no fresh French rolls, only slices of stale graham bread from yesterday, the most detestable of bread so far as I was concerned.

"Nothing was delivered this morning, sir," Brown started to explain apologetically; but I interrupted him.

"The paper?"

"Yes, sir, it was delivered, but it was the only thing, and it is the last time, too. There won't be any paper to-morrow. The paper says so. Can I send out and get you some condensed milk?"

I shook my head, accepted the coffee black, and spread open the paper. The headlines explained everything, explained too much, in fact, for the lengths of pessimism to which the journal went were ridiculous. A general strike, it said, had been called all over the United States; and most foreboding anxieties were expressed concerning the provisioning of the great cities.

I read on hastily, skimming much and remembering much of labour troubles in the past. For a generation the general strike had been the dream of organized labour, which dream had arisen originally in the mind of Debs, one of the great labour leaders of thirty years before. I recollected that in my young college-settlement days I had even written an article on the subject for one of the magazines and that I had entitled it "The Dream of Debs." And I must confess that I had treated the idea very cavalierly and academically as a dream and nothing more. Time and the world had rolled on, Gompers was gone, the American Federation of Labour was gone, and gone was Debs with all his wild revolutionary ideas; but the dream had persisted, and here it was at last realized in fact. But I laughed, as I read, at the journal's gloomy outlook. I knew better. I had seen organized labour worsted in too many conflicts. It would be a matter only of days when the thing would be settled. This was a national strike, and it wouldn't take the Government long to break it.

I threw the paper down and proceeded to dress. It would certainly be interesting to be out in the streets of San Francisco when not a wheel was turning and the whole city was taking an enforced vacation.

"I beg your pardon, sir," Brown said, as he handed me my cigar-case, "but Mr. Harmmed has asked to see you before you go out."

"Send him in right away," I answered.

Harmmed was the butler. When he entered I could see he was labouring under controlled excitement. He came at once to the point.

"What shall I do, sir? There will be needed provisions, and the delivery drivers are on strike. And the electricity is shut off—I guess they're on strike, too."

"Are the shops open?" I asked.

"Only the small ones, sir. The retail clerks are out, and the big ones can't open; but the owners and their families are running the little ones themselves."

"Then take the machine," I said, "and go the rounds and make your purchases. Buy plenty of everything you need or may need. Get a box of candles, no, get half-a-dozen boxes. And, when you're done, tell Harrison to bring the machine around to the club for me, not later than eleven."

Harmmed shook his head gravely. "Mr. Harrison has struck along with the Chauffeurs' Union, and I don't know how to run the machine myself."

"Oh, ho, he has, has he?" said. "Well, when next Mister Harrison happens around you tell him that he can look elsewhere for a position."

"Yes, sir."

"You don't happen to belong to a Butlers' Union, do you, Harmmed?"

"No, sir," was the answer. "And even if I did I'd not desert my employer in a crisis like this. No, sir, I would—"

"All right, thank you," I said. "Now you get ready to accompany me. I'll run the machine myself, and we'll lay in a stock of provisions to stand a siege."

It was a beautiful first of May, even as May days go. The sky was cloudless, there was no wind, and the air was warm—almost balmy. Many autos were out, but the owners were driving them themselves. The streets were crowded but quiet. The working class, dressed in its Sunday best, was out taking the air and observing the effects of the strike. It was all so unusual, and withal so peaceful, that I found myself enjoying it. My nerves were tingling with mild excitement. It was a sort of placid adventure. I passed Miss Chickering. She was at the helm of her little runabout. She swung around and came after me, catching me at the corner.

"Oh, Mr. Corf!"' she hailed. "Do you know where I can buy candles? I've been to a dozen shops, and they're all sold out. It's dreadfully awful, isn't it?"

But her sparkling eyes gave the lie to her words. Like the rest of us, she was enjoying it hugely. Quite an adventure it was, getting those candles. It was not until we went across the city and down into the working-class quarter south of Market Street that we found small corner groceries that had not yet sold out. Miss Chickering thought one box was sufficient, but I persuaded her into taking four. My car was large, and I laid in a dozen boxes. There was no telling what delays might arise in the settlement of the strike. Also, I filled the car with sacks of flour, baking-powder, tinned goods, and all the ordinary necessaries of life suggested by Harmmed, who fussed around and clucked over the purchases like an anxious old hen.

The remarkable thing, that first day of the strike, was that no one really apprehended anything serious. The announcement of organized labour in the morning papers that it was prepared to stay out a month or three months was laughed at. And yet that very first day we might have guessed as much from the fact that the working class took practically no part in the great rush to buy provisions. Of course not. For weeks and months, craftily and secretly, the whole working class had been laying in private stocks of provisions. That was why we were permitted to go down and buy out the little groceries in the working-class neighbourhoods.

It was not until I arrived at the club that afternoon that I began to feel the first alarm. Everything was in confusion. There were no olives for the cocktails, and the service was by hitches and jerks. Most of the men were angry, and all were worried. A babel of voices greeted me as I entered. General Folsom, nursing his capacious paunch in a window-seat in the smoking-room was defending himself against half-a-dozen excited gentlemen who were demanding that he should do something.

"What can I do more than I have done?" he was saying. "There are no orders from Washington. If you gentlemen will get a wire through I'll do anything I am commanded to do. But I don't see what can be done. The first thing I did this morning, as soon as I learned of the strike, was to order in the troops from the Presidio, three thousand of them. They're guarding the banks, the Mint, the post office, and all the public buildings. There is no disorder whatever. The strikers are keeping the peace perfectly. You can't expect me to shoot them down as they walk along the streets with wives and children all in their best bib and tucker."

"I'd like to know what's happening on Wall Street," I heard Jimmy Wombold say as I passed along. I could imagine his anxiety, for I knew that he was deep in the big Consolidated-Western deal.

"Say, Corf," Atkinson bustled up to me, "is your machine running?"

"Yes," I answered, "but what's the matter with your own?"

"Broken down, and the garages are all closed. And my wife's somewhere around Truckee, I think, stalled on the overland. Can't get a wire to her for love or money. She should have arrived this evening. She may be starving. Lend me your machine."

"Can't get it across the bay," Halstead spoke up. "The ferries aren't running. But I tell you what you can do. There's Rollinson, oh, Rollinson, come here a moment. Atkinson wants to get a machine across the bay. His wife is stuck on the overland at Truckee. Can't you bring the Lurlette across from Tiburon and carry the machine over for him?"

The Lurlette was a two-hundred-ton, ocean-going schooner-yacht.

Rollinson shook his head. "You couldn't get a longshoreman to land the machine on board, even if I could get the Lurlette over, which I can't, for the crew are members of the Coast Seamen's Union, and they're on strike along with the rest."

"But my wife may be starving," I could hear Atkinson wailing as I moved on.

At the other end of the smoking-room I ran into a group of men bunched excitedly and angrily around Bertie Messener. And Bertie was stirring them up and prodding them in his cool, cynical way. Bertie didn't care about the strike. He didn't care much about anything. He was blasé, at least in all the clean things of life; the nasty things had no attraction for him. He was worth twenty millions, all of it in safe investments, and he had never done a tap of productive work in his life, inherited it all from his father and two uncles. He had been everywhere, seen everything, and done everything but get married, and this last in the face of the grim and determined attack of a few hundred ambitious mammas. For years he had been the greatest catch, and as yet he had avoided being caught. He was disgracefully eligible. On top of his wealth he was young, handsome, and, as I said before, clean. He was a great athlete, a young blond god that did everything perfectly and admirably with the solitary exception of matrimony. And he didn't care about anything, had no ambitions, no passions, no desire to do the very things he did so much better than other men.

"This is sedition!" one man in the group was crying. Another called it revolt and revolution, and another called it anarchy.

"I can't see it," Bertie said. "I have been out in the streets all morning. Perfect order reigns. I never saw a more law-abiding populace. There's no use calling it names. It's not any of those things. It's just what it claims to be, a general strike, and it's your turn to play, gentlemen."

"And we'll play all right!" cried Garfield, one of the traction millionaires. "We'll show this dirt where its place is—the beasts! Wait till the Government takes a hand."

"But where is the Government?" Bertie interposed. "It might as well be at the bottom of the sea so far as you're concerned. You don't know what's happening at Washington. You don't know whether you've got a Government or not."

"Don't you worry about that," Garfield blurted out.

"I assure you I'm not worrying," Bertie smiled languidly. "But it seems to me it's what you fellows are doing. Look in the glass, Garfield."

Garfield did not look, but had he looked he would have seen a very excited gentleman with rumpled, iron-grey hair, a flushed face, mouth sullen and vindictive, and eyes wildly gleaming.

"It's not right, I tell you," little Hanover said; and from his tone I was sure that he had already said it a number of times.

"Now that's going too far, Hanover," Bertie replied. "You fellows make me tired. You're all open-shop men. You've eroded my eardrums with your endless gabble for the open shop and the right of a man to work. You've harangued along those lines for years. Labour is doing nothing wrong in going out on this general strike. It is violating no law of God nor man. Don't you talk, Hanover. You've been ringing the changes too long on the God-given right to work . . . or not to work; you can't escape the corollary. It's a dirty little sordid scrap, that's all the whole thing is. You've got labour down and gouged it, and now labour's got you down and is gouging you, that's all, and you're squealing."

Every man in the group broke out in indignant denials that labour had ever been gouged.

"No, sir!" Garfield was shouting. "We've done the best for labour. Instead of gouging it, we've given it a chance to live. We've made work for it. Where would labour be if it hadn't been for us?"

"A whole lot better off," Bertie sneered. "You've got labour down and gouged it every time you got a chance, and you went out of your way to make chances."

"No! No!" were the cries.

"There was the teamsters' strike, right here in San Francisco," Bertie went on imperturbably. "The Employers' Association precipitated that strike. You know that. And you know I know it, too, for I've sat in these very rooms and heard the inside talk and news of the fight. First you precipitated the strike, then you bought the Mayor and the Chief of Police and broke the strike. A pretty spectacle, you philanthropists getting the teamsters down and gouging them.

"Hold on, I'm not through with you. It's only last year that the labour ticket of Colorado elected a governor. He was never seated. You know why. You know how your brother philanthropists and capitalists of Colorado worked it. It was a case of getting labour down and gouging it. You kept the president of the South-western Amalgamated Association of Miners in jail for three years on trumped-up murder charges, and with him out of the way you broke up the association. That was gouging labour, you'll admit. The third time the graduated income tax was declared unconstitutional was a gouge. So was the eight-hour Bill you killed in the last Congress.

"And of all unmitigated immoral gouges, your destruction of the closed-shop principle was the limit. You know how it was done. You bought out Farburg, the last president of the old American Federation of Labour. He was your creature—or the creature of all the trusts and employers' associations, which is the same thing. You precipitated the big closed-shop strike. Farburg betrayed that strike. You won, and the old American Federation of Labour crumbled to pieces. You follows destroyed it, and by so doing undid yourselves; for right on top of it began the organization of the I.L.W.—the biggest and solidest organization of labour the United States has ever seen, and you are responsible for its existence and for the present general strike. You smashed all the old federations and drove labour into the I.L.W., and the I.L.W. called the general strike—still fighting for the closed shop. And then you have the effrontery to stand here face to face and tell me that you never got labour down and gouged it. Bah!"

This time there were no denials. Garfield broke out in self-defence—

"We've done nothing we were not compelled to do, if we were to win."

"I'm not saying anything about that," Bertie answered. "What I am complaining about is your squealing now that you're getting a taste of your own medicine. How many strikes have you won by starving labour into submission? Well, labour's worked out a scheme whereby to starve you into submission. It wants the closed shop, and, if it can get it by starving you, why, starve you shall."

"I notice that you have profited in the past by those very labour gouges you mention," insinuated Brentwood, one of the wiliest and most astute of our corporation lawyers. "The receiver is as bad as the thief," he sneered. "You had no hand in the gouging, but you took your whack out of the gouge."

"That is quite beside the question, Brentwood," Bertie drawled. "You're as bad as Hanover, intruding the moral element. I haven't said that anything is right or wrong. It's all a rotten game, I know; and my sole kick is that you fellows are squealing now that you're down and labour's taking a gouge out of you. Of course I've taken the profits from the gouging and, thanks to you, gentlemen, without having personally to do the dirty work. You did that for me, oh, believe me, not because I am more virtuous than you, but because my good father and his various brothers left me a lot of money with which to pay for the dirty work."

"If you mean to insinuate—" Brentwood began hotly.

"Hold on, don't get all-ruffled up," Bertie interposed insolently. "There's no use in playing hypocrites in this thieves' den. The high and lofty is all right for the newspapers, boys' clubs, and Sunday schools—that's part of the game; but for heaven's sake don't let's play it on one another. You know, and you know that I know just what jobbery was done in the building trades' strike last fall, who put up the money, who did the work, and who profited by it." (Brentwood flushed darkly.) "But we are all tarred with the same brush, and the best thing for us to do is to leave morality out of it. Again I repeat, play the game, play it to the last finish, but for goodness' sake don't squeal when you get hurt."

When I left the group Bertie was off on a new tack tormenting them with the more serious aspects of the situation, pointing out the shortage of supplies that was already making itself felt, and asking them what they were going to do about it. A little later I met him in the cloak-room, leaving, and gave him a lift home in my machine.

"It's a great stroke, this general strike," he said, as we bowled along through the crowded but orderly streets. "It's a smashing body-blow. Labour caught us napping and struck at our weakest place, the stomach. I'm going to get out of San Francisco, Corf. Take my advice and get out, too. Head for the country, anywhere. You'll have more chance. Buy up a stock of supplies and get into a tent or a cabin somewhere. Soon there'll be nothing but starvation in this city for such as we."

How correct Bertie Messener was I never dreamed. I decided that he was an alarmist. As for myself, I was content to remain and watch the fun. After I dropped him, instead of going directly home, I went on in a hunt for more food. To my surprise, I learned that the small groceries where I had bought in the morning were sold out. I extended my search to the Potrero, and by good luck managed to pick up another box of candles, two sacks of wheat flour, ten pounds of graham flour (which would do for the servants), a case of tinned corn, and two cases of tinned tomatoes. It did look as though there was going to be at least a temporary food shortage, and I hugged myself over the goodly stock of provisions I had laid in.

The next morning I had my coffee in bed as usual, and, more than the cream, I missed the daily paper. It was this absence of knowledge of what was going on in the world that I found the chief hardship. Down at the club there was little news. Rider had crossed from Oakland in his launch, and Halstead had been down to San Jose and back in his machine. They reported the same conditions in those places as in San Francisco. Everything was tied up by the strike. All grocery stocks had been bought out by the upper classes. And perfect order reigned. But what was happening over the rest of the country—in Chicago? New York? Washington? Most probably the same things that were happening with us, we concluded; but the fact that we did not know with absolute surety was irritating.

General Folsom had a bit of news. An attempt had been made to place army telegraphers in the telegraph offices, but the wires had been cut in every direction. This was, so far, the one unlawful act committed by labour, and that it was a concerted act he was fully convinced. He had communicated by wireless with the army post at Benicia, the telegraph lines were even then being patrolled by soldiers all the way to Sacramento. Once, for one short instant, they had got the Sacramento call, then the wires, somewhere, were cut again. General Folsom reasoned that similar attempts to open communication were being made by the authorities all the way across the continent, but he was non-committal as to whether or not he thought the attempt would succeed. What worried him was the wire-cutting; he could not but believe that it was an important part of the deep-laid labour conspiracy. Also, he regretted that the Government had not long since established its projected chain of wireless stations.

The days came and went, and for a while it was a humdrum time. Nothing happened. The edge of excitement had become blunted. The streets were not so crowded. The working class did not come uptown any more to see how we were taking the strike. And there were not so many automobiles running around. The repair-shops and garages were closed, and whenever a machine broke down it went out of commission. The clutch on mine broke, and neither love nor money could get it repaired. Like the rest, I was now walking. San Francisco lay dead, and we did not know what was happening over the rest of the country. But from the very fact that we did not know we could conclude only that the rest of the country lay as dead as San Francisco. From time to time the city was placarded with the proclamations of organized labour, these had been printed months before, and evidenced how thoroughly the I.L.W. had prepared for the strike. Every detail had been worked out long in advance. No violence had occurred as yet, with the exception of the shooting of a few wire-cutters by the soldiers, but the people of the slums were starving and growing ominously restless.

The business men, the millionaires, and the professional class held meetings and passed resolutions, but there was no way of making the proclamations public. They could not even get them printed. One result of these meetings, however, was that General Folsom was persuaded into taking military possession of the wholesale houses and of all the flour, grain, and food warehouses. It was high time, for suffering was becoming acute in the homes of the rich, and bread-lines were necessary. I knew that my servants were beginning to draw long faces, and it was amazing, the hole they made in my stock of provisions. In fact, as I afterward surmised, each servant was stealing from me and secreting a private stock of provisions for himself.

But with the formation of the bread-lines came new troubles. There was only so much of a food reserve in San Francisco, and at the best it could not last long. Organized labour, we knew, had its private supplies; nevertheless, the whole working class joined the bread-lines. As a result, the provisions General Folsom had taken possession of diminished with perilous rapidity. How were the soldiers to distinguish between a shabby middle-class man, a member of the I.L.W., or a slum dweller? The first and the last had to be fed, but the soldiers did not know all the I.L.W. men in the city, much less the wives and sons and daughters of the I.L.W. men. The employers helping, a few of the known union men were flung out of the bread-lines; but that amounted to nothing. To make matters worse, the Government tugs that had been hauling food from the army depots on Mare Island to Angel Island found no more food to haul. The soldiers now received their rations from the confiscated provisions, and they received them first.

The beginning of the end was in sight. Violence was beginning to show its face. Law and order were passing away, and passing away, I must confess, among the slum people and the upper classes. Organized labour still maintained perfect order. It could well afford to, it had plenty to eat. I remember the afternoon at the club when I caught Halstead and Brentwood whispering in a corner. They took me in on the venture. Brentwood's machine was still in running order, and they were going out cow-stealing. Halstead had a long butcher knife and a cleaver. We went out to the outskirts of the city. Here and there were cows grazing, but always they were guarded by their owners. We pursued our quest, following along the fringe of the city to the east, and on the hills near Hunter's Point we came upon a cow guarded by a little girl. There was also a young calf with the cow. We wasted no time on preliminaries. The little girl ran away screaming, while we slaughtered the cow. I omit the details, for they are not nice, we were unaccustomed to such work, and we bungled it.

But in the midst of it, working with the haste of fear, we heard cries, and we saw a number of men running toward us. We abandoned the spoils and took to our heels. To our surprise we were not pursued. Looking back, we saw the men hurriedly cutting up the cow. They had been on the same lay as ourselves. We argued that there was plenty for all, and ran back. The scene that followed beggars description. We fought and squabbled over the division like savages. Brentwood, I remember, was a perfect brute, snarling and snapping and threatening that murder would be done if we did not get our proper share.

And we were getting our share when there occurred a new irruption on the scene. This time it was the dreaded peace officers of the I.L.W. The little girl had brought them. They were armed with whips and clubs, and there were a score of them. The little girl danced up and down in anger, the tears streaming down her cheeks, crying: "Give it to 'em! Give it to 'em! That guy with the specs, he did it! Mash his face for him! Mash his face!" That guy with the specs was I, and I got my face mashed, too, though I had the presence of mind to take off my glasses at the first. My! but we did receive a trouncing as we scattered in all directions. Brentwood, Halstead, and I fled away for the machine. Brentwood's nose was bleeding, while Halstead's cheek was cut across with the scarlet slash of a black-snake whip.

And, lo, when the pursuit ceased and we had gained the machine, there, hiding behind it, was the frightened calf. Brentwood warned us to be cautious, and crept up on it like a wolf or tiger. Knife and cleaver had been left behind, but Brentwood still had his hands, and over and over on the ground he rolled with the poor little calf as he throttled it. We threw the carcass into the machine, covered it over with a robe, and started for home. But our misfortunes had only begun. We blew out a tyre. There was no way of fixing it, and twilight was coming on. We abandoned the machine, Brentwood pulling and staggering along in advance, the calf, covered by the robe, slung across his shoulders. We took turn about carrying that calf, and it nearly killed us. Also, we lost our way. And then, after hours of wandering and toil, we encountered a gang of hoodlums. They were not I.L.W. men, and I guess they were as hungry as we. At any rate, they got the calf and we got the thrashing. Brentwood raged like a madman the rest of the way home, and he looked like one, with his torn clothes, swollen nose, and blackened eyes.

There wasn't any more cow-stealing after that. General Folsom sent his troopers out and confiscated all the cows, and his troopers, aided by the militia, ate most of the meat. General Folsom was not to be blamed; it was his duty to maintain law and order, and he maintained it by means of the soldiers, wherefore he was compelled to feed them first of all.

It was about this time that the great panic occurred. The wealthy classes precipitated the flight, and then the slum people caught the contagion and stampeded wildly out of the city. General Folsom was pleased. It was estimated that at least 200,000 had deserted San Francisco, and by that much was his food problem solved. Well do I remember that day. In the morning I had eaten a crust of bread. Half of the afternoon I had stood in the bread-line; and after dark I returned home, tired and miserable, carrying a quart of rice and a slice of bacon. Brown met me at the door. His face was worn and terrified. All the servants had fled, he informed me. He alone remained. I was touched by his faithfulness and, when I learned that he had eaten nothing all day, I divided my food with him. We cooked half the rice and half the bacon, sharing it equally and reserving the other half for morning. I went to bed with my hunger, and tossed restlessly all night. In the morning I found Brown had deserted me, and, greater misfortune still, he had stolen what remained of the rice and bacon.

It was a gloomy handful of men that came together at the club that morning. There was no service at all. The last servant was gone. I noticed, too, that the silver was gone, and I learned where it had gone. The servants had not taken it, for the reason, I presume, that the club members got to it first. Their method of disposing of it was simple. Down south of Market Street, in the dwellings of the I.L.W., the housewives had given square meals in exchange for it. I went back to my house. Yes, my silver was gone, all but a massive pitcher. This I wrapped up and carried down south of Market Street.

I felt better after the meal, and returned to the club to learn if there was anything new in the situation. Hanover, Collins, and Dakon were just leaving. There was no one inside, they told me, and they invited me to come along with them. They were leaving the city, they said, on Dakon's horses, and there was a spare one for me. Dakon had four magnificent carriage horses that he wanted to save, and General Folsom had given him the tip that next morning all the horses that remained in the city were to be confiscated for food. There were not many horses left, for tens of thousands of them had been turned loose into the country when the hay and grain gave out during the first days. Birdall, I remember, who had great draying interests, had turned loose three hundred dray horses. At an average value of five hundred dollars, this had amounted to $150,000. He had hoped, at first, to recover most of the horses after the strike was over, but in the end he never recovered one of them. They were all eaten by the people that fled from San Francisco. For that matter, the killing of the army mules and horses for food had already begun.

Fortunately for Dakon, he had had a plentiful supply of hay and grain stored in his stable. We managed to raise four saddles, and we found the animals in good condition and spirited, withal unused to being ridden. I remembered the San Francisco of the great earthquake as we rode through the streets, but this San Francisco was vastly more pitiable. No cataclysm of nature had caused this, but, rather, the tyranny of the labour unions. We rode down past Union Square and through the theatre, hotel, and shopping districts. The streets were deserted. Here and there stood automobiles, abandoned where they had broken down or when the gasolene had given out. There was no sign of life, save for the occasional policemen and the soldiers guarding the banks and public buildings. Once we came upon an I.L.W. man pasting up the latest proclamation. We stopped to read. "We have maintained an orderly strike," it ran; "and we shall maintain order to the end. The end will come when our demands are satisfied, and our demands will be satisfied when we have starved our employers into submission, as we ourselves in the past have often been starved into submission."

"Messener's very words," Collins said. "And I, for one, am ready to submit, only they won't give me a chance to submit. I haven't had a full meal in an age. I wonder what horse-meat tastes like?"

We stopped to read another proclamation: "When we think our employers are ready to submit we shall open up the telegraphs and place the employers' associations of the United States in communication. But only messages relating to peace terms shall be permitted over the wires."

We rode on, crossed Market Street, and a little later were passing through the working-class district. Here the streets were not deserted. Leaning over the gates or standing in groups were the I.L.W. men. Happy, well-fed children were playing games, and stout housewives sat on the front steps gossiping. One and all cast amused glances at us. Little children ran after us, crying: "Hey, mister, ain't you hungry?" And one woman, nursing a child at her breast, called to Dakon: "Say, Fatty, I'll give you a meal for your skate, ham and potatoes, currant jelly, white bread, canned butter, and two cups of coffee."

"Have you noticed, the last few days," Hanover remarked to me, "that there's not been a stray dog in the streets?"

I had noticed, but I had not thought about it before. It was high time to leave the unfortunate city. We at last managed to connect with the San Bruno Road, along which we headed south. I had a country place near Menlo, and it was our objective. But soon we began to discover that the country was worse off and far more dangerous than the city. There the soldiers and the I.L.W. kept order; but the country had been turned over to anarchy. Two hundred thousand people had fled from San Francisco, and we had countless evidences that their flight had been like that of an army of locusts.

They had swept everything clean. There had been robbery and fighting. Here and there we passed bodies by the roadside and saw the blackened ruins of farm-houses. The fences were down, and the crops had been trampled by the feet of a multitude. All the vegetable patches had been rooted up by the famished hordes. All the chickens and farm animals had been slaughtered. This was true of all the main roads that led out of San Francisco. Here and there, away from the roads, farmers had held their own with shotguns and revolvers, and were still holding their own. They warned us away and refused to parley with us. And all the destruction and violence had been done by the slum-dwellers and the upper classes. The I.L.W. men, with plentiful food supplies, remained quietly in their homes in the cities.

Early in the ride we received concrete proof of how desperate was the situation. To the right of us we heard cries and rifle-shots. Bullets whistled dangerously near. There was a crashing in the underbrush; then a magnificent black truck-horse broke across the road in front of us and was gone. We had barely time to notice that he was bleeding and lame. He was followed by three soldiers. The chase went on among the trees on the left. We could hear the soldiers calling to one another. A fourth soldier limped out upon the road from the right, sat down on a boulder, and mopped the sweat from his face.

"Militia," Dakon whispered. "Deserters."

The man grinned up at us and asked for a match. In reply to Dakon's "What's the word?" he informed us that the militiamen were deserting. "No grub," he explained. "They're feedin' it all to the regulars." We also learned from him that the military prisoners had been released from Alcatraz Island because they could no longer be fed.

I shall never forget the next sight we encountered. We came upon it abruptly around a turn of the road. Overhead arched the trees. The sunshine was filtering down through the branches. Butterflies were fluttering by, and from the fields came the song of larks. And there it stood, a powerful touring car. About it and in it lay a number of corpses. It told its own tale. Its occupants, fleeing from the city, had been attacked and dragged down by a gang of slum dwellers, hoodlums. The thing had occurred within twenty-four hours. Freshly opened meat and fruit tins explained the reason for the attack. Dakon examined the bodies.

"I thought so," he reported. "I've ridden in that car. It was Perriton, the whole family. We've got to watch out for ourselves from now on."

"But we have no food with which to invite attack," I objected.

Dakon pointed to the horse I rode, and I understood.

Early in the day Dakon's horse had cast a shoe. The delicate hoof had split, and by noon the animal was limping. Dakon refused to ride it farther, and refused to desert it. So, on his solicitation, we went on. He would lead the horse and join us at my place. That was the last we saw of him; nor did we ever learn his end.

By one o'clock we arrived at the town of Menlo, or, rather, at the site of Menlo, for it was in ruins. Corpses lay everywhere. The business part of the town, as well as part of the residences, had been gutted by fire. Here and there a residence still held out; but there was no getting near them. When we approached too closely we were fired upon. We met a woman who was poking about in the smoking ruins of her cottage. The first attack, she told us had been on the stores, and as she talked we could picture that raging, roaring, hungry mob flinging itself on the handful of townspeople. Millionaires and paupers had fought side by side for the food, and then fought with one another after they got it. The town of Palo Alto and Stanford University had been sacked in similar fashion, we learned. Ahead of us lay a desolate, wasted land; and we thought we were wise in turning off to my place. It lay three miles to the west, snuggling among the first rolling swells of the foothills.

But as we rode along we saw that the devastation was not confined to the main roads. The van of the flight had kept to the roads, sacking the small towns as it went; while those that followed had scattered out and swept the whole countryside like a great broom. My place was built of concrete, masonry, and tiles, and so had escaped being burned, but it was gutted clean. We found the gardener's body in the windmill, littered around with empty shot-gun shells. He had put up a good fight. But no trace could we find of the two Italian labourers, nor of the house-keeper and her husband. Not a live thing remained. The calves, the colts, all the fancy poultry and thoroughbred stock, everything, was gone. The kitchen and the fireplaces, where the mob had cooked, were a mess, while many camp-fires outside bore witness to the large number that had fed and spent the night. What they had not eaten they had carried away. There was not a bite for us.

We spent the rest of the night vainly waiting for Dakon, and in the morning, with our revolvers, fought off half-a-dozen marauders. Then we killed one of Dakon's horses, hiding for the future what meat we did not immediately eat. In the afternoon Collins went out for a walk, but failed to return. This was the last straw to Hanover. He was for flight there and then, and I had great difficulty in persuading him to wait for daylight. As for myself, I was convinced that the end of the general strike was near, and I was resolved to return to San Francisco. So, in the morning, we parted company, Hanover heading south, fifty pounds of horse-meat strapped to his saddle, while I, similarly loaded, headed north. Little Hanover pulled through all right, and to the end of his life he will persist, I know, in boring everybody with the narrative of his subsequent adventures.

I got as far as Belmont, on the main road back, when I was robbed of my horse-meat by three militiamen. There was no change in the situation, they said, except that it was going from bad to worse. The I.L.W. had plenty of provisions hidden away and could last out for months. I managed to get as far as Baden, when my horse was taken away from me by a dozen men. Two of them were San Francisco policemen, and the remainder were regular soldiers. This was ominous. The situation was certainly extreme when the regulars were beginning to desert. When I continued my way on foot, they already had the fire started, and the last of Dakon's horses lay slaughtered on the ground.

As luck would have it, I sprained my ankle, and succeeded in getting no farther than South San Francisco. I lay there that night in an out-house, shivering with the cold and at the same time burning with fever. Two days I lay there, too sick to move, and on the third, reeling and giddy, supporting myself on an extemporized crutch, I tottered on toward San Francisco. I was weak as well, for it was the third day since food had passed my lips. It was a day of nightmare and torment. As in a dream I passed hundreds of regular soldiers drifting along in the opposite direction, and many policemen, with their families, organized in large groups for mutual protection.

As I entered the city I remembered the workman's house at which I had traded the silver pitcher, and in that direction my hunger drove me. Twilight was falling when I came to the place. I passed around by the alleyway and crawled up the black steps, on which I collapsed. I managed to reach out with the crutch and knock on the door. Then I must have fainted, for I came to in the kitchen, my face wet with water, and whisky being poured down my throat. I choked and spluttered and tried to talk. I began saying something about not having any more silver pitchers, but that I would make it up to them afterward if they would only give me something to eat. But the housewife interrupted me.

"Why, you poor man," she said, "haven't you heard? The strike was called off this afternoon. Of course we'll give you something to eat."

She bustled around, opening a tin of breakfast bacon and preparing to fry it.

"Let me have some now, please," I begged; and I ate the raw bacon on a slice of bread, while her husband explained that the demands of the I.L.W. had been granted. The wires had been opened up in the early afternoon, and everywhere the employers' associations had given in. There hadn't been any employers left in San Francisco, but General Folsom had spoken for them. The trains and steamers would start running in the morning, and so would everything else just as soon as system could be established.

And that was the end of the general strike. I never want to see another one. It was worse than a war. A general strike is a cruel and immoral thing, and the brain of man should be capable of running industry in a more rational way. Harrison is still my chauffeur. It was part of the conditions of the I.L.W. that all of its members should be reinstated in their old positions. Brown never came back, but the rest of the servants are with me. I hadn't the heart to discharge them, poor creatures, they were pretty hard-pressed when they deserted with the food and silver. And now I can't discharge them. They have all been unionized by the I.L.W. The tyranny of organized labour is getting beyond human endurance. Something must be done.

THE SEA-FARMER

"That wull be the doctor's launch," said Captain MacElrath.

The pilot grunted, while the skipper swept on with his glass from the launch to the strip of beach and to Kingston beyond, and then slowly across the entrance to Howth Head on the northern side.

"The tide's right, and we'll have you docked in two hours," the pilot vouchsafed, with an effort at cheeriness. "Ring's End Basin, is it?"

This time the skipper grunted.

"A dirty Dublin day."

Again the skipper grunted. He was weary with the night of wind in the Irish Channel behind him, the unbroken hours of which he had spent on the bridge. And he was weary with all the voyage behind him, two years and four months between home port and home port, eight hundred and fifty days by his log.

"Proper wunter weather," he answered, after a silence. "The town is undistinct. Ut wull be rainun' guid an' hearty for the day."

Captain MacElrath was a small man, just comfortably able to peep over the canvas dodger of the bridge. The pilot and third officer loomed above him, as did the man at the wheel, a bulky German, deserted from a warship, whom he had signed on in Rangoon. But his lack of inches made Captain MacElrath a no less able man. At least so the Company reckoned, and so would he have reckoned could he have had access to the carefully and minutely compiled record of him filed away in the office archives. But the Company had never given him a hint of its faith in him. It was not the way of the Company, for the Company went on the principle of never allowing an employee to think himself indispensable or even exceedingly useful; wherefore, while quick to censure, it never praised. What was Captain MacElrath, anyway, save a skipper, one skipper of the eighty-odd skippers that commanded the Company's eighty-odd freighters on all the highways and byways of the sea?

Beneath them, on the main deck, two Chinese stokers were carrying breakfast for'ard across the rusty iron plates that told their own grim story of weight and wash of sea. A sailor was taking down the life-line that stretched from the forecastle, past the hatches and cargo-winches, to the bridge-deck ladder.

"A rough voyage," suggested the pilot.

"Aye, she was fair smokin' ot times, but not thot I minded thot so much as the lossin' of time. I hate like onythun' tull loss time."

So saying, Captain MacElrath turned and glanced aft, aloft and alow, and the pilot, following his gaze, saw the mute but convincing explanation of that loss of time. The smoke-stack, buff-coloured underneath, was white with salt, while the whistle-pipe glittered crystalline in the random sunlight that broke for the instant through a cloud-rift. The port lifeboat was missing, its iron davits, twisted and wrenched, testifying to the mightiness of the blow that had been struck the old Tryapsic. The starboard davits were also empty. The shattered wreck of the lifeboat they had held lay on the fiddley beside the smashed engine-room skylight, which was covered by a tarpaulin. Below, to star-board, on the bridge deck, the pilot saw the crushed mess-room door, roughly bulkheaded against the pounding seas. Abreast of it, on the smokestack guys, and being taken down by the bos'n and a sailor, hung the huge square of rope netting which had failed to break those seas of their force.

"Twice afore I mentioned thot door tull the owners," said Captain MacElrath. "But they said ut would do. There was bug seas thot time. They was uncreditable bug. And thot buggest one dud the domage. Ut fair carried away the door an' laid ut flat on the mess table an' smashed out the chief's room. He was a but sore about ut."

"It must 'a' been a big un," the pilot remarked sympathetically.

"Aye, ut was thot. Thungs was lively for a but. Ut finished the mate. He was on the brudge wuth me, an' I told hum tull take a look tull the wedges o' number one hatch. She was takin' watter freely an' I was no sure o' number one. I dudna like the look o' ut, an' I was fuggerin' maybe tull heave to tull the marn, when she took ut over abaft the brudge. My word, she was a bug one. We got a but of ut ourselves on the brudge. I dudna miss the mate ot the first, what o' routin' out Chips an' bulkheadun' thot door an' stretchun' the tarpaulin over the sky-light. Then he was nowhere to be found. The men ot the wheel said as he seen hum goin' down the lodder just afore she hut us. We looked for'ard, we looked tull hus room, aye looked tull the engine-room, an' we looked along aft on the lower deck, and there he was, on both sides the cover to the steam-pipe runnun' tull the after-wunches."

The pilot ejaculated an oath of amazement and horror.

"Aye," the skipper went on wearily, "an' on both sides the steam-pipe uz well. I tell ye he was in two pieces, splut clean uz a herrin'. The sea must a-caught hum on the upper brudge deck, carried hum clean across the fiddley, an' banged hum head-on tull the pipe cover. It sheered through hum like so much butter, down atween the eyes, an' along the middle of hum, so that one leg an' arm was fast tull the one piece of hum, an' one leg an' arm fast tull the other piece of hum. I tull ye ut was fair grewsome. We putt hum together an' rolled hum in canvas uz we pulled hum out."

The pilot swore again.

"Oh, ut wasna onythun' tull greet about," Captain MacElrath assured him. "'Twas a guid ruddance. He was no a sailor, thot mate-fellow. He was only fut for a pugsty, an' a dom puir apology for thot same."

It is said that there are three kinds of Irish, Catholic, Protestant, and North-of-Ireland, and that the North-of-Ireland Irishman is a transplanted Scotchman. Captain MacElrath was a North-of-Ireland man, and, talking for much of the world like a Scotchman, nothing aroused his ire quicker than being mistaken for a Scotchman. Irish he stoutly was, and Irish he stoutly abided, though it was with a faint lip-lift of scorn that he mentioned mere South-of-Ireland men, or even Orange-men. Himself he was Presbyterian, while in his own community five men were all that ever mustered at a meeting in the Orange Men's Hall. His community was the Island McGill, where seven thousand of his kind lived in such amity and sobriety that in the whole island there was but one policeman and never a public-house at all.

Captain MacElrath did not like the sea, and had never liked it. He wrung his livelihood from it, and that was all the sea was, the place where he worked, as the mill, the shop, and the counting-house were the places where other men worked. Romance never sang to him her siren song, and Adventure had never shouted in his sluggish blood. He lacked imagination. The wonders of the deep were without significance to him. Tornadoes, hurricanes, waterspouts, and tidal waves were so many obstacles to the way of a ship on the sea and of a master on the bridge, they were that to him, and nothing more. He had seen, and yet not seen, the many marvels and wonders of far lands. Under his eyelids burned the brazen glories of the tropic seas, or ached the bitter gales of the North Atlantic or far South Pacific; but his memory of them was of mess-room doors stove in, of decks awash and hatches threatened, of undue coal consumption, of long passages, and of fresh paint-work spoiled by unexpected squalls of rain.

"I know my buzz'ness," was the way he often put it, and beyond his business was all that he did not know, all that he had seen with the mortal eyes of him and yet that he never dreamed existed. That he knew his business his owners were convinced, or at forty he would not have held command of the Tryapsic, three thousand tons net register, with a cargo capacity of nine thousand tons and valued at fifty-thousand pounds.

He had taken up seafaring through no love of it, but because it had been his destiny, because he had been the second son of his father instead of the first. Island McGill was only so large, and the land could support but a certain definite proportion of those that dwelt upon it. The balance, and a large balance it was, was driven to the sea to seek its bread. It had been so for generations. The eldest sons took the farms from their fathers; to the other sons remained the sea and its salt-ploughing. So it was that Donald MacElrath, farmer's son and farm-boy himself, had shifted from the soil he loved to the sea he hated and which it was his destiny to farm. And farmed it he had, for twenty years, shrewd, cool-headed, sober, industrious, and thrifty, rising from ship's boy and forecastle hand to mate and master of sailing-ships and thence into steam, second officer, first, and master, from small command to larger, and at last to the bridge of the old Tryapsic, old, to be sure, but worth her fifty thousand pounds and still able to bear up in all seas, and weather her nine thousand tons of freight.

From the bridge of the Tryapsic, the high place he had gained in the competition of men, he stared at Dublin harbour opening out, at the town obscured by the dark sky of the dreary wind-driven day, and at the tangled tracery of spars and rigging of the harbour shipping. Back from twice around the world he was, and from interminable junketings up and down on far stretches, home-coming to the wife he had not seen in eight-and-twenty months, and to the child he had never seen and that was already walking and talking. He saw the watch below of stokers and trimmers bobbing out of the forecastle doors like rabbits from a warren and making their way aft over the rusty deck to the mustering of the port doctor. They were Chinese, with expressionless, Sphinx-like faces, and they walked in peculiar shambling fashion, dragging their feet as if the clumsy brogans were too heavy for their lean shanks.

He saw them and he did not see them, as he passed his hand beneath his visored cap and scratched reflectively his mop of sandy hair. For the scene before him was but the background in his brain for the vision of peace that was his, a vision that was his often during long nights on the bridge when the old Tryapsic wallowed on the vexed ocean floor, her decks awash, her rigging thrumming in the gale gusts or snow squalls or driving tropic rain. And the vision he saw was of farm and farm-house and straw-thatched outbuildings, of children playing in the sun, and the good wife at the door, of lowing kine, and clucking fowls, and the stamp of horses in the stable, of his father's farm next to him, with, beyond, the woodless, rolling land and the hedged fields, neat and orderly, extending to the crest of the smooth, soft hills. It was his vision and his dream, his Romance and Adventure, the goal of all his effort, the high reward for the salt-ploughing and the long, long furrows he ran up and down the whole world around in his farming of the sea.

In simple taste and homely inclination this much-travelled map was more simple and homely than the veriest yokel. Seventy-one years his father was, and had never slept a night out of his own bed in his own house on Island McGill. That was the life ideal, so Captain MacElrath considered, and he was prone to marvel that any man, not under compulsion, should leave a farm to go to sea. To this much-travelled man the whole world was as familiar as the village to the cobbler sitting in his shop. To Captain MacElrath the world was a village. In his mind's eye he saw its streets a thousand leagues long, aye, and longer; turnings that doubled earth's stormiest headlands or were the way to quiet inland ponds; cross-roads, taken one way, that led to flower-lands and summer seas, and that led the other way to bitter, ceaseless gales and the perilous bergs of the great west wind drift. And the cities, bright with lights, were as shops on these long streets, shops where business was transacted, where bunkers were replenished, cargoes taken or shifted, and orders received from the owners in London town to go elsewhere and beyond, ever along the long sea-lanes, seeking new cargoes here, carrying new cargoes there, running freights wherever shillings and pence beckoned and underwriters did not forbid. But it was all a weariness to contemplate, and, save that he wrung from it his bread, it was without profit under the sun.

The last good-bye to the wife had been at Cardiff, twenty-eight months before, when he sailed for Valparaiso with coals, nine thousand tons and down to his marks. From Valparaiso he had gone to Australia, light, a matter of six thousand miles on end with a stormy passage and running short of bunker coal. Coals again to Oregon, seven thousand miles, and nigh as many more with general cargo for Japan and China. Thence to Java, loading sugar for Marseilles, and back along the Mediterranean to the Black Sea, and on to Baltimore, down to her marks with crome ore, buffeted by hurricanes, short again of bunker coal and calling at Bermuda to replenish. Then a time charter, Norfolk, Virginia, loading mysterious contraband coal and sailing for South Africa under orders of the mysterious German supercargo put on board by the charterers. On to Madagascar, steaming four knots by the supercargo's orders, and the suspicion forming that the Russian fleet might want the coal. Confusion and delays, long waits at sea, international complications, the whole world excited over the old Tryapsic and her cargo of contraband, and then on to Japan and the naval port of Sassebo. Back to Australia, another time charter and general merchandise picked up at Sydney, Melbourne, and Adelaide, and carried on to Mauritius, Lourenço Marques, Durban, Algoa Bay, and Cape Town. To Ceylon for orders, and from Ceylon to Rangoon to load rice for Rio Janeiro. Thence to Buenos Aires and loading maize for the United Kingdom or the Continent, stopping at St. Vincent, to receive orders to proceed to Dublin. Two years and four months, eight hundred and fifty days by the log, steaming up and down the thousand-league-long sea-lanes and back again to Dublin town. And he was well aweary.

A little tug had laid hold of the Tryapsic, and with clang and clatter and shouted command, with engines half-ahead, slow-speed, or half-astern, the battered old sea-tramp was nudged and nosed and shouldered through the dock-gates into Ring's End Basin. Lines were flung ashore, fore and aft, and a 'midship spring got out. Already a small group of the happy shore-staying folk had clustered on the dock.

"Ring off," Captain MacElrath commanded in his slow thick voice; and the third officer worked the lever of the engine-room telegraph.

"Gangway out!" called the second officer; and when this was accomplished, "That will do."

It was the last task of all, gangway out. "That will do" was the dismissal. The voyage was ended, and the crew shambled eagerly forward across the rusty decks to where their sea-bags were packed and ready for the shore. The taste of the land was strong in the men's mouths, and strong it was in the skipper's mouth as he muttered a gruff good day to the departing pilot, and himself went down to his cabin. Up the gangway were trooping the customs officers, the surveyor, the agent's clerk, and the stevedores. Quick work disposed of these and cleared his cabin, the agent waiting to take him to the office.

"Dud ye send word tull the wife?" had been his greeting to the clerk.

"Yes, a telegram, as soon as you were reported."

"She'll likely be comin' down on the marnin' train," the skipper had soliloquized, and gone inside to change his clothes and wash.

He took a last glance about the room and at two photographs on the wall, one of the wife the other of an infant, the child he had never seen. He stepped out into the cabin, with its panelled walls of cedar and maple, and with its long table that seated ten, and at which he had eaten by himself through all the weary time. No laughter and clatter and wordy argument of the mess-room had been his. He had eaten silently, almost morosely, his silence emulated by the noiseless Asiatic who had served him. It came to him suddenly, the overwhelming realization of the loneliness of those two years and more. All his vexations and anxieties had been his own. He had shared them with no one. His two young officers were too young and flighty, the mate too stupid. There was no consulting with them. One tenant had shared the cabin with him, that tenant his responsibility. They had dined and supped together, walked the bridge together, and together they had bedded.

"Och!" he muttered to that grim companion, "I'm quit of you, an' wull quit . . . for a wee."

Ashore he passed the last of the seamen with their bags, and, at the agent's, with the usual delays, put through his ship business. When asked out by them to drink he took milk and soda.

"I am no teetotaler," he explained; "but for the life o' me I canna bide beer or whusky."

In the early afternoon, when he finished paying off his crew, he hurried to the private office where he had been told his wife was waiting.

His eyes were for her first, though the temptation was great to have more than a hurried glimpse of the child in the chair beside her. He held her off from him after the long embrace, and looked into her face long and steadily, drinking in every feature of it and wondering that he could mark no changes of time. A warm man, his wife thought him, though had the opinion of his officers been asked it would have been: a harsh man and a bitter one.

"Wull, Annie, how is ut wi' ye?" he queried, and drew her to him again.

And again he held her away from him, this wife of ten years and of whom he knew so little. She was almost a stranger, more a stranger than his Chinese steward, and certainly far more a stranger than his own officers whom he had seen every day, day and day, for eight hundred and fifty days. Married ten years, and in that time he had been with her nine weeks, scarcely a honeymoon. Each time home had been a getting acquainted again with her. It was the fate of the men who went out to the salt-ploughing. Little they knew of their wives and less of their children. There was his chief engineer, old, near-sighted MacPherson, who told the story of returning home to be locked out of his house by his four-year kiddie that never had laid eyes on him before.

"An' thus 'ull be the loddie," the skipper said, reaching out a hesitant hand to the child's cheek.

But the boy drew away from him, sheltering against the mother's side.

"Och!" she cried, "and he doesna know his own father."

"Nor I hum. Heaven knows I could no a-picked hum out of a crowd, though he'll be havin' your nose I'm thunkun'."

"An' your own eyes, Donald. Look ut them. He's your own father, laddie. Kiss hum like the little mon ye are."

But the child drew closer to her, his expression of fear and distrust growing stronger, and when the father attempted to take him in his arms he threatened to cry.

The skipper straightened up, and to conceal the pang at his heart he drew out his watch and looked at it.

"Ut's time to go, Annie," he said. "Thot train 'ull be startun'."

He was silent on the train at first, divided between watching the wife with the child going to sleep in her arms and looking out of the window at the tilled fields and green unforested hills vague and indistinct in the driving drizzle that had set in. They had the compartment to themselves. When the boy slept she laid him out on the seat and wrapped him warmly. And when the health of relatives and friends had been inquired after, and the gossip of Island McGill narrated, along with the weather and the price of land and crops, there was little left to talk about save themselves, and Captain

MacElrath took up the tale brought home for the good wife from all his world's-end wandering. But it was not a tale of marvels he told, nor of beautiful flower-lands nor mysterious Eastern cities.

"What like is Java?" she asked once.

"Full o' fever. Half the crew down wuth ut an' luttle work. Ut was quinine an' quinine the whole blessed time. Each marnun' 'twas quinine an' gin for all hands on an empty stomach. An' they who was no sick made ut out to be hovun' ut bad uz the rest."

Another time she asked about Newcastle.

"Coals an' coal-dust, thot's all. No a nice sutty. I lost two Chinks there, stokers the both of them. An' the owners paid a fine tull the Government of a hundred pounds each for them. 'We regret tull note,' they wrut me, I got the letter tull Oregon, 'We regret tull note the loss o' two Chinese members o' yer crew ot Newcastle, an' we recommend greater carefulness un the future.' Greater carefulness! And I could no a-been more careful. The Chinks hod forty-five pounds each comun' tull them in wages, an' I was no a-thunkun' they 'ud run.

"But thot's their way—'we regret tull note,' 'we beg tull advise,' 'we recommend,' 'we canna understand'—an' the like o' thot. Domned cargo tank! An' they would thunk I could drive her like a Lucania, an' wi'out burnun' coals. There was thot propeller. I was after them a guid while for ut. The old one was iron, thuck on the edges, an' we couldna make our speed. An' the new one was bronze—nine hundred pounds ut cost, an' then wantun' their returns out o' ut, an' me wuth a bod passage an' lossin' time every day. 'We regret tull note your long passage from Voloparaiso tull Sydney wuth an average daily run o' only one hundred an' suxty-seven. We hod expected better results wuth the new propeller. You should a-made an average daily run o' two hundred and suxteen.'

"An' me on a wunter passage, blowin' a luvin' gale half the time, wuth hurricane force in atweenwhiles, an' hove to sux days, wuth engines stopped an' bunker coal runnun' short, an' me wuth a mate thot stupid he could no pass a shup's light ot night wi'out callun' me tull the brudge. I wrut an' told 'em so. An' then: 'Our nautical adviser suggests you kept too far south,' an' 'We are lookun' for better results from thot propeller.' Nautical adviser!—shore pilot! Ut was the regular latitude for a wunter passage from Voloparaiso tull Sydney.

"An' when I come un tull Auckland short o' coal, after lettun' her druft sux days wuth the fires out tull save the coal, an' wuth only twenty tons in my bunkers, I was thunkun' o' the lossin' o' time an' the expense, an' tull save the owners I took her un an' out wi'out pilotage. Pilotage was no compulsory. An' un Yokohama, who should I meet but Captun Robinson o' the Dyapsic. We got a-talkun' about ports an' places down Australia-way, an' first thing he says: 'Speakun' o' Auckland—of course, Captun, you was never un Auckland?' 'Yus,' I says, 'I was un there very recent.' 'Oh, ho,' he says, very angry-like, 'so you was the smart Aleck thot fetched me thot letter from the owners: "We note item of fufteen pounds for pilotage ot Auckland. A shup o' ours was un tull Auckland recently an' uncurred no such charge. We beg tull advise you thot we conseeder thus pilotage an onnecessary expense which should no be uncurred un the future."'

"But dud they say a word tull me for the fufteen pounds I saved tull them? No a word. They send a letter tull Captun Robinson for no savun' them the fufteen pounds, an' tull me: 'We note item of two guineas doctor's fee at Auckland for crew. Please explain thus onusual expunditure.' Ut was two o' the Chinks. I was thunkun' they hod beri-beri, an' thot was the why o' sendun' for the doctor. I buried the two of them ot sea not a week after. But ut was: 'Please explain thus onusual expunditure,' an' tull Captun Robinson, 'We beg tull advise you thot we conseeder thus pilotage an onnecessary expense.'

"Dudna I cable them from Newcastle, tellun' them the old tank was thot foul she needed dry-dock? Seven months out o' dry-dock, an' the West Coast the quickest place for foulun' un the world. But freights was up, an' they hod a charter o' coals for Portland. The Arrata, one o' the Woor Line, left port the same day uz us, bound for Portland, an' the old Tryapsic makun' sux knots, seven ot the best. An' ut was ot Comox, takun' un bunker coal, I got the letter from the owners. The boss humself hod signed ut, an' ot the bottom he wrut un hus own bond: 'The Arrata beat you by four an' a half days. Am dusappointed.' Dusappointed! When I had cabled them from Newcastle. When she drydocked ot Portland, there was whuskers on her a foot long, barnacles the size o' me fust, oysters like young sauce plates. Ut took them two days afterward tull clean the dock o' shells an' muck.

"An' there was the motter o' them fire-bars ot Newcastle. The firm ashore made them heavier than the engineer's speecifications, an' then forgot tull charge for the dufference. Ot the last moment, wuth me ashore gettun' me clearance, they come wuth the bill: 'Tull error on fire-bars, sux pounds.' They'd been tull the shup an' MacPherson hod O.K.'d ut. I said ut was strange an' would no pay. 'Then you are dootun' the chief engineer,' says they. 'I'm no dootun',' says I, 'but I canna see my way tull sign. Come wuth me tull the shup. The launch wull cost ye naught an' ut 'ull brung ye back. An' we wull see what MacPherson says.'

"But they would no come. Ot Portland I got the bill un a letter. I took no notice. Ot Hong-Kong I got a letter from the owners. The bill hod been sent tull them. I wrut them from Java explainun'. At Marseilles the owners wrut me: 'Tull extra work un engine-room, sux pounds. The engineer has O.K.'d ut, an' you have no O.K.'d ut. Are you dootun' the engineer's honesty?' I wrut an' told them I was no dootun' his honesty; thot the bill was for extra weight o' fire-bars; an' thot ut was O.K. Dud they pay ut? They no dud. They must unvestigate. An' some clerk un the office took sick, an' the bill was lost. An' there was more letters. I got letters from the owners an' the firm—'Tull error on fire-bars, sux pounds'—ot Baltimore, ot Delagoa Bay, ot Moji, ot Rangoon, ot Rio, an' ot Montevuddio. Ut uz no settled yut. I tell ye, Annie, the owners are hard tull please."

He communed with himself for a moment, and then muttered indignantly: "Tull error on fire-bars, sux pounds."

"Hov ye heard of Jamie?" his wife asked in the pause.

Captain MacElrath shook his head.

"He was washed off the poop wuth three seamen."

"Whereabouts?"

"Off the Horn. 'Twas on the Thornsby."

"They would be runnun' homeward bound?"

"Aye," she nodded. "We only got the word three days gone. His wife is greetin' like tull die."

"A good lod, Jamie," he commented, "but a stiff one ot carryun' on. I mind me when we was mates together un the Abion. An' so Jamie's gone."

Again a pause fell, to be broken by the wife.

"An' ye will no a-heard o' the Bankshire? MacDougall lost her in Magellan Straits. 'Twas only yesterday ut was in the paper."

"A cruel place, them Magellan Straits," he said. "Dudna thot domned mate-fellow nigh putt me ashore twice on the one passage through? He was a eediot, a lunatuc. I wouldna have hum on the brudge a munut. Comun' tull Narrow Reach, thuck weather, wuth snow squalls, me un the chart-room, dudna I guv hum the changed course? 'South-east-by-east,' I told hum. 'South-east-by-east, sir,' says he. Fufteen munuts after I comes on tull the brudge. 'Funny,' says thot mate-fellow, 'I'm no rememberun' ony islands un the mouth o' Narrow Reach. I took one look ot the islands an' yells, 'Putt your wheel hard a-starboard,' tull the mon ot the wheel. An' ye should a-seen the old Tryapsic turnun' the sharpest circle she ever turned. I waited for the snow tull clear, an' there was Narrow Reach, nice uz ye please, tull the east'ard an' the islands un the mouth o' False Bay tull the south'ard. 'What course was ye steerun'?' I says tull the mon ot the wheel. 'South-by-east, sir,' says he. I looked tull the mate-fellow. What could I say? I was thot wroth I could a-kult hum. Four points dufference. Five munuts more an' the old Tryapsic would a-been funushed."

"An' was ut no the same when we cleared the Straits tull the east'ard? Four hours would a-seen us guid an' clear. I was forty hours then on the brudge. I guv the mate his course, an' the bearun' o' the Askthar Light astern. 'Don't let her bear more tull the north'ard than west-by-north,' I said tull hum, 'an' ye wull be all right.' An' I went below an' turned un. But I couldna sleep for worryun'. After forty hours on the brudge, what was four hours more? I thought. An' for them four hours wull ye be lettun' the mate loss her on ye? 'No,' I says to myself. An' wuth thot I got up, hod a wash an' a cup o' coffee, an' went tull the brudge. I took one look ot the bearun' o' Askthar Light. 'Twas nor'west-by-west, and the old Tryapsic down on the shoals. He was a eediot, thot mate-fellow. Ye could look overside an' see the duscoloration of the watter. 'Twas a close call for the old Tryapsic I'm tellun' ye. Twice un thirty hours he'd a-hod her ashore uf ut hod no been for me."

Captain MacElrath fell to gazing at the sleeping child with mild wonder in his small blue eyes, and his wife sought to divert him from his woes.

"Ye remember Jummy MacCaul?" she asked. "Ye went tull school wuth hus two boys. Old Jummy MacCaul thot hoz the farm beyond Doctor Haythorn's place."

"Oh, aye, an' what o' hum? Uz he dead?"

"No, but he was after askun' your father, when he sailed last time for Voloparaiso, uf ye'd been there afore. An' when your father says no, then Jummy says, 'An' how wull he be knowun a' tull find hus way?' An' with thot your father says: 'Verry sumple ut uz, Jummy. Supposun' you was goin' tull the mainland tull a mon who luved un Belfast. Belfast uz a bug sutty, Jummy, an' how would ye be findun' your way?' 'By way o' me tongue,' says Jummy; 'I'd be askun' the folk I met.' 'I told ye ut was sumple,' says your father. 'Ut's the very same way my Donald finds the road tull Voloparaiso. He asks every shup he meets upon the sea tull ot last he meets wuth a shup thot's been tull Voloparaiso, an' the captun o' thot shup tells hum the way.' An' Jummy scratches hus head an' says he understands an' thot ut's a very sumple motter after all."

The skipper chuckled at the joke, and his tired blue eyes were merry for the moment.

"He was a thun chap, thot mate-fellow, oz thun oz you an' me putt together," he remarked after a time, a slight twinkle in his eye of appreciation of the bull. But the twinkle quickly disappeared and the blue eyes took on a bleak and wintry look. "What dud he do ot Voloparaiso but land sux hundred fathom o' chain cable an' take never a receipt from the lighter-mon. I was gettun' my clearance ot the time. When we got tull sea, I found he hod no receipt for the cable.

"'An' ye no took a receipt for ut?' says I.

"'No,' says he. 'Wasna ut goin' direct tull the agents?'

"'How long ha' ye been goin' tull sea,' says I, 'not tull be knowin' the mate's duty uz tull deluver no cargo wuthout receipt for same? An' on the West Coast ot thot. What's tull stop the lighter-mon from stealun' a few lengths o' ut?'

"An' ut come out uz I said. Sux hundred hundred went over the side, but four hundred an' ninety-five was all the agents received. The lighter-mon swore ut was all he received from the mate—four hundred an' ninety-five fathom. I got a letter from the owners ot Portland. They no blamed the mate for ut, but me, an' me ashore ot the time on shup's buzz'ness. I could no be in the two places ot the one time. An' the letters from the owners an' the agents uz still comun' tull me.

"Thot mate-fellow was no a proper sailor, an' no a mon tull work for owners. Dudna he want tull break me wuth the Board of Trade for bein' below my marks? He said as much tull the bos'n. An' he told me tull my face homeward bound thot I'd been half an inch under my marks. 'Twas at Portland, loadun' cargo un fresh watter an' goin' tull Comox tull load bunker coal un salt watter. I tell ye, Annie, ut takes close fuggerin', an' I was half an inch under the load-line when the bunker coal was un. But I'm no tellun' any other body but you. An' thot mate-fellow untendun' tull report me tull the Board o' Trade, only for thot he saw fut tull be sliced un two pieces on the steam-pipe cover.

"He was a fool. After loadun' ot Portland I hod tull take on suxty tons o' coal tull last me tull Comox. The charges for lighterun' was heavy, an' no room ot the coal dock. A French barque was lyin' alongside the dock an' I spoke tull the captun, askun' hum what he would charge when work for the day was done, tull haul clear for a couple o' hours an' let me un. 'Twenty dollars,' said he. Ut was savun' money on lighters tull the owner, an' I gave ut tull hum. An' thot night, after dark, I hauled un an' took on the coal. Then I started tull go out un the stream an' drop anchor—under me own steam, of course.

"We hod tull go out stern first, an' somethun' went wrong wuth the reversun' gear. Old MacPherson said he could work ut by hond, but very slow ot thot. An' I said 'All right.' We started. The pilot was on board. The tide was ebbun' stuffly, an' right abreast an' a but below was a shup lyin' wuth a lighter on each side. I saw the shup's ridun' lights, but never a light on the lighters. Ut was close quarters to shuft a bug vessel onder steam, wuth MacPherson workun' the reversun' gear by hond. We hod to come close down upon the shup afore I could go ahead an' clear o' the shups on the dock-ends. An' we struck the lighter stern-on, just uz I rung tull MacPherson half ahead.

"'What was thot?' says the pilot, when we struck the lighter.

"'I dunna know,' says I, 'an' I'm wonderun'.'

"The pilot was no keen, ye see, tull hus job. I went on tull a guid place an' dropped anchor, an' ut would all a-been well but for thot domned eediot mate.

"'We smashed thot lighter,' says he, comun' up the lodder tull the brudge—an' the pilot stondun' there wuth his ears cocked tull hear.

"'What lighter?' says I.

"'Thot lighter alongside the shup,' says the mate.

"'I dudna see no lighter,' says I, and wuth thot I steps on hus fut guid an' hard.

"After the pilot was gone I says tull the mate: 'Uf you dunna know onythun', old mon, for Heaven's sake keep your mouth shut.'

"'But ye dud smash thot lighter, dudn't ye?' says he.

"'Uf we dud,' says I, 'ut's no your buzz'ness tull be tellun' the pilot, though, mind ye, I'm no admuttun' there was ony lighter.'

"An' next marnun', just uz I'm after dressun', the steward says, 'A mon tull see ye, sir.' 'Fetch hum un,' says I. An' un he come. 'Sut down,' says I. An' he sot down.

"He was the owner of the lighter, an' when he hod told hus story, I says, 'I dudna see ony lighter.'

"'What, mon?' says he. 'No see a two-hundred-ton lighter, bug oz a house, alongside thot shup?'

"'I was goin' by the shup's lights,' says I, 'an' I dudna touch the shup, thot I know.'

"'But ye dud touch the lighter,' says he. 'Ye smashed her. There's a thousand dollars' domage done, an' I'll see ye pay for ut.'

"'Look here, muster,' says I, 'when I'm shuftun' a shup ot night I follow the law, an' the law dustunctly says I must regulate me actions by the lights o' the shuppun'. Your lighter never hod no ridun' light, nor dud I look for ony lighter wuthout lights tull show ut.'

"'The mate says—' he beguns.

"'Domn the mate,' says I. 'Dud your lighter hov a ridun' light?'

"'No, ut dud not,' says he, 'but ut was a clear night wuth the moon a-showun'.'

"'Ye seem tull know your buzz'ness,' says I. 'But let me tell ye thot I know my buzz'ness uz well, an' thot I'm no a-lookun' for lighters wuthout lights. Uf ye thunk ye hov a case, go ahead. The steward will show ye out. Guid day.'

"An' thot was the end o' ut. But ut wull show ye what a puir fellow thot mate was. I call ut a blessun' for all masters thot he was sliced un two on thot steam-pipe cover. He had a pull un the office an' thot was the why he was kept on."

"The Wekley farm wull soon be for sale, so the agents be tellun' me," his wife remarked, slyly watching what effect her announcement would have upon him.

His eyes flashed eagerly on the instant, and he straightened up as might a man about to engage in some agreeable task. It was the farm of his vision, adjoining his father's, and her own people farmed not a mile away.

"We wull be buyun' ut," he said, "though we wull be no tellun' a soul of ut ontul ut's bought an' the money paid down. I've savun' consuderable these days, though pickun's uz no what they used to be, an' we hov a tidy nest-egg laid by. I wull see the father an' hove the money ready tull hus hond, so uf I'm ot sea he can buy whenever the land offers."

He rubbed the frosted moisture from the inside of the window and peered out at the pouring rain, through which he could discern nothing.

"When I was a young men I used tull be afeard thot the owners would guv me the sack. Stull afeard I am of the sack. But once thot farm is mine I wull no be afeard ony longer. Ut's a puir job thus sea-farmun'. Me managin' un all seas an' weather an' perils o' the deep a shup worth fufty thousand pounds, wuth cargoes ot times worth fufty thousand more, a hundred thousand pounds, half a million dollars uz the Yankees say, an' me wuth all the responsubility gettun' a screw o' twenty pounds a month. What mon ashore, managin' a buz'ness worth a hundred thousand pounds wull be gettun' uz small a screw uz twenty pounds? An' wuth such masters uz a captun serves, the owners, the underwriters, an' the Board o' Trade, all pullun' an wantun' dufferent thungs, the owners wantun' quick passages an' domn the rusk, the underwriters wantun' safe passages an' domn the delay, an' the Board o' Trade wantun' cautious passages an' caution always meanun' delay. Three dufferent masters, an' all three able an' wullun' to break ye uf ye don't serve their dufferent wushes."

He felt the train slackening speed, and peered again through the misty window. He stood up, buttoned his overcoat, turned up the collar, and awkwardly gathered the child, still asleep, in his arms.

"I wull see the father," he said, "an' hov the money ready tull hus hond so uf I'm ot sea when the land offers he wull no muss the chance tull buy. An' then the owners can guv me the sack uz soon uz they like. Ut will be all night un, an' I wull be wuth you, Annie, an' the sea can go tull hell."

Happiness was in both their faces at the prospect, and for a moment both saw the same vision of peace. Annie leaned toward him, and as the train stopped they kissed each other across the sleeping child.

SAMUEL

Margaret Henan would have been a striking figure under any circumstances, but never more so than when I first chanced upon her, a sack of grain of fully a hundredweight on her shoulder, as she walked with sure though tottering stride from the cart-tail to the stable, pausing for an instant to gather strength at the foot of the steep steps that led to the grain-bin. There were four of these steps, and she went up them, a step at a time, slowly, unwaveringly, and with so dogged certitude that it never entered my mind that her strength could fail her and let that hundred-weight sack fall from the lean and withered frame that well nigh doubled under it. For she was patently an old woman, and it was her age that made me linger by the cart and watch.

Six times she went between the cart and the stable, each time with a full sack on her back, and beyond passing the time of day with me she took no notice of my presence. Then, the cart empty, she fumbled for matches and lighted a short clay pipe, pressing down the burning surface of the tobacco with a calloused and apparently nerveless thumb. The hands were noteworthy. They were large-knuckled, sinewy and malformed by labour, rimed with callouses, the nails blunt and broken, and with here and there cuts and bruises, healed and healing, such as are common to the hands of hard-working men. On the back were huge, upstanding veins, eloquent of age and toil. Looking at them, it was hard to believe that they were the hands of the woman who had once been the belle of Island McGill. This last, of course, I learned later. At the time I knew neither her history nor her identity.

She wore heavy man's brogans. Her legs were stockingless, and I had noticed when she walked that her bare feet were thrust into the crinkly, iron-like shoes that sloshed about her lean ankles at every step. Her figure, shapeless and waistless, was garbed in a rough man's shirt and in a ragged flannel petticoat that had once been red. But it was her face, wrinkled, withered and weather-beaten, surrounded by an aureole of unkempt and straggling wisps of greyish hair, that caught and held me. Neither drifted hair nor serried wrinkles could hide the splendid dome of a forehead, high and broad without verging in the slightest on the abnormal.

The sunken cheeks and pinched nose told little of the quality of the life that flickered behind those clear blue eyes of hers. Despite the minutiæ of wrinkle-work that somehow failed to weazen them, her eyes were clear as a girl's, clear, out-looking, and far-seeing, and with an open and unblinking steadfastness of gaze that was disconcerting. The remarkable thing was the distance between them. It is a lucky man or woman who has the width of an eye between, but with Margaret Henan the width between her eyes was fully that of an eye and a half. Yet so symmetrically moulded was her face that this remarkable feature produced no uncanny effect, and, for that matter, would have escaped the casual observer's notice. The mouth, shapeless and toothless, with down-turned corners and lips dry and parchment-like, nevertheless lacked the muscular slackness so usual with age. The lips might have been those of a mummy, save for that impression of rigid firmness they gave. Not that they were atrophied. On the contrary, they seemed tense and set with a muscular and spiritual determination. There, and in the eyes, was the secret of the certitude with which she carried the heavy sacks up the steep steps, with never a false step or overbalance, and emptied them in the grain-bin.

"You are an old woman to be working like this," I ventured.

She looked at me with that strange, unblinking gaze, and she thought and spoke with the slow deliberateness that characterized everything about her, as if well aware of an eternity that was hers and in which there was no need for haste. Again I was impressed by the enormous certitude of her. In this eternity that seemed so indubitably hers, there was time and to spare for safe-footing and stable equilibrium, for certitude, in short. No more in her spiritual life than in carrying the hundredweights of grain was there a possibility of a misstep or an overbalancing. The feeling produced in me was uncanny. Here was a human soul that, save for the most glimmering of contacts, was beyond the humanness of me. And the more I learned of Margaret Henan in the weeks that followed the more mysteriously remote she became. She was as alien as a far-journeyer from some other star, and no hint could she nor all the countryside give me of what forms of living, what heats of feeling, or rules of philosophic contemplation actuated her in all that she had been and was.

"I wull be suvunty-two come Guid Friday a fortnight," she said in reply to my question.

"But you are an old woman to be doing this man's work, and a strong man's work at that," I insisted.

Again she seemed to immerse herself in that atmosphere of contemplative eternity, and so strangely did it affect me that I should not have been surprised to have awaked a century or so later and found her just beginning to enunciate her reply—

"The work hoz tull be done, an' I am beholden tull no one."

"But have you no children, no family, relations?"

"Oh, aye, a-plenty o' them, but they no see fut tull be helpun' me."

She drew out her pipe for a moment, then added, with a nod of her head toward the house, "I luv' wuth meself."

I glanced at the house, straw-thatched and commodious, at the large stable, and at the large array of fields I knew must belong with the place.

"It is a big bit of land for you to farm by yourself."

"Oh, aye, a bug but, suvunty acres. Ut kept me old mon buzzy, along wuth a son an' a hired mon, tull say naught o' extra honds un the harvest an' a maid-servant un the house."

She clambered into the cart, gathered the reins in her hands, and quizzed me with her keen, shrewd eyes.

"Belike ye hail from over the watter—Ameruky, I'm meanun'?"

"Yes, I'm a Yankee," I answered.

"Ye wull no be findun' mony Island McGill folk stoppun' un Ameruky?"

"No; I don't remember ever meeting one, in the States."

She nodded her head.

"They are home-luvun' bodies, though I wull no be sayin' they are no fair-travelled. Yet they come home ot the last, them oz are no lost ot sea or kult by fevers an' such-like un foreign parts."

"Then your sons will have gone to sea and come home again?" I queried.

"Oh, aye, all savun' Samuel oz was drownded."

At the mention of Samuel I could have sworn to a strange light in her eyes, and it seemed to me, as by some telepathic flash, that I divined in her a tremendous wistfulness, an immense yearning. It seemed to me that here was the key to her inscrutableness, the clue that if followed properly would make all her strangeness plain. It came to me that here was a contact and that for the moment I was glimpsing into the soul of her. The question was tickling on my tongue, but she forestalled me.

She tchk'd to the horse, and with a "Guid day tull you, sir," drove off.

A simple, homely people are the folk of Island McGill, and I doubt if a more sober, thrifty, and industrious folk is to be found in all the world. Meeting them abroad—and to meet them abroad one must meet them on the sea, for a hybrid seafaring and farmer breed are they—one would never take them to be Irish. Irish they claim to be, speaking of the North of Ireland with pride and sneering at their Scottish brothers; yet Scotch they undoubtedly are, transplanted Scotch of long ago, it is true, but none the less Scotch, with a thousand traits, to say nothing of their tricks of speech and woolly utterance, which nothing less than their Scotch clannishness could have preserved to this late day.

A narrow loch, scarcely half a mile wide, separates Island McGill from the mainland of Ireland; and, once across this loch, one finds himself in an entirely different country. The Scotch impression is strong, and the people, to commence with, are Presbyterians. When it is considered that there is no public-house in all the island and that seven thousand souls dwell therein, some idea may be gained of the temperateness of the community. Wedded to old ways, public opinion and the ministers are powerful influences, while fathers and mothers are revered and obeyed as in few other places in this modern world. Courting lasts never later than ten at night, and no girl walks out with her young man without her parents' knowledge and consent.

The young men go down to the sea and sow their wild oats in the wicked ports, returning periodically, between voyages, to live the old intensive morality, to court till ten o'clock, to sit under the minister each Sunday, and to listen at home to the same stern precepts that the elders preached to them from the time they were laddies. Much they learned of women in the ends of the earth, these seafaring sons, yet a canny wisdom was theirs and they never brought wives home with them. The one solitary exception to this had been the schoolmaster, who had been guilty of bringing a wife from half a mile the other side of the loch. For this he had never been forgiven, and he rested under a cloud for the remainder of his days. At his death the wife went back across the loch to her own people, and the blot on the escutcheon of Island McGill was erased. In the end the sailor-men married girls of their own homeland and settled down to become exemplars of all the virtues for which the island was noted.

Island McGill was without a history. She boasted none of the events that go to make history. There had never been any wearing of the green, any Fenian conspiracies, any land disturbances. There had been but one eviction, and that purely technical, a test case, and on advice of the tenant's lawyer. So Island McGill was without annals. History had passed her by. She paid her taxes, acknowledged her crowned rulers, and left the world alone; all she asked in return was that the world should leave her alone. The world was composed of two parts, Island McGill and the rest of it. And whatever was not Island McGill was outlandish and barbarian; and well she knew, for did not her seafaring sons bring home report of that world and its ungodly ways?

It was from the skipper of a Glasgow tramp, as passenger from Colombo to Rangoon, that I had first learned of the existence of Island McGill; and it was from him that I had carried the letter that gave me entrance to the house of Mrs. Ross, widow of a master mariner, with a daughter living with her and with two sons, master mariners themselves and out upon the sea. Mrs. Ross did not take in boarders, and it was Captain Ross's letter alone that had enabled me to get from her bed and board. In the evening, after my encounter with Margaret Henan, I questioned Mrs. Ross, and I knew on the instant that I had in truth stumbled upon mystery.

Like all Island McGill folk, as I was soon to discover, Mrs. Ross was at first averse to discussing Margaret Henan at all. Yet it was from her I learned that evening that Margaret Henan had once been one of the island belles. Herself the daughter of a well-to-do farmer, she had married Thomas

Henan, equally well-to-do. Beyond the usual housewife's tasks she had never been accustomed to work. Unlike many of the island women, she had never lent a hand in the fields.

"But what of her children?" I asked.

"Two o' the sons, Jamie an' Timothy uz married an' be goun' tull sea. Thot bug house close tull the post office uz Jamie's. The daughters thot ha' no married be luvun' wuth them as dud marry. An' the rest be dead."

"The Samuels," Clara interpolated, with what I suspected was a giggle.

She was Mrs. Ross's daughter, a strapping young woman with handsome features and remarkably handsome black eyes.

"'Tuz naught to be smuckerun' ot," her mother reproved her.

"The Samuels?" I intervened. "I don't understand."

"Her four sons thot died."

"And were they all named Samuel?"

"Aye."

"Strange," I commented in the lagging silence.

"Very strange," Mrs. Ross affirmed, proceeding stolidly with the knitting of the woollen singlet on her knees, one of the countless under-garments that she interminably knitted for her skipper sons.

"And it was only the Samuels that died?" I queried, in further attempt.

"The others luved," was the answer. "A fine fomuly, no finer on the island. No better lods ever sailed out of Island McGill. The munuster held them up oz models tull pottern after. Nor was ever a whusper breathed again' the girls."

"But why is she left alone now in her old age?" I persisted. "Why don't her own flesh and blood look after her? Why does she live alone? Don't they ever go to see her or care for her?"

"Never a one un twenty years an' more now. She fetched ut on tull herself. She drove them from the house just oz she drove old Tom Henan, thot was her husband, tull hus death."

"Drink?" I ventured.

Mrs. Ross shook her head scornfully, as if drink was a weakness beneath the weakest of Island McGill.

A long pause followed, during which Mrs. Ross knitted stolidly on, only nodding permission when Clara's young man, mate on one of the Shire Line sailing ships, came to walk out with her. I studied the half-dozen ostrich eggs, hanging in the corner against the wall like a cluster of some monstrous fruit. On each shell were painted precipitous and impossible seas through which full-rigged ships foamed with a lack of perspective only equalled by their sharp technical perfection. On the mantelpiece stood two large pearl shells, obviously a pair, intricately carved by the patient hands of New Caledonian convicts. In the centre of the mantel was a stuffed bird-of-paradise, while about the room were scattered gorgeous shells from the southern seas, delicate sprays of coral sprouting from barnacled pi-pi shells and cased in glass, assegais from South Africa, stone axes from New Guinea, huge Alaskan tobacco-pouches beaded with heraldic totem designs, a boomerang from Australia, divers ships in glass bottles, a cannibal kai-kai bowl from the Marquesas, and fragile cabinets from China and the Indies and inlaid with mother-of-pearl and precious woods.

I gazed at this varied trove brought home by sailor sons, and pondered the mystery of Margaret Henan, who had driven her husband to his death and been forsaken by all her kin. It was not the drink. Then what was it? some shocking cruelty? some amazing infidelity? or some fearful, old-world peasant-crime?

I broached my theories, but to all Mrs. Ross shook her head.

"Ut was no thot," she said. "Margaret was a guid wife an' a guid mother, an' I doubt she would harm a fly. She brought up her fomuly God-fearin' an' decent-minded. Her trouble was thot she took lunatic—turned eediot."

Mrs. Ross tapped significantly on her forehead to indicate a state of addlement.

"But I talked with her this afternoon," I objected, "and I found her a sensible woman, remarkably bright for one of her years."

"Aye, an' I'm grantun' all thot you say," she went on calmly. "But I am no referrun' tull thot. I am referrun' tull her wucked-headed an' vucious stubbornness. No more stubborn woman ever luv'd than Margaret Henan. Ut was all on account o' Samuel, which was the name o' her youngest an' they do say her favourut brother, hum oz died by hus own hond all through the munuster's mustake un no registerun' the new church ot Dublin. Ut was a lesson thot the name was musfortunate, but she would no take ut, an' there was talk when she called her first child Samuel—hum thot died o' the croup. An' wuth thot what does she do but call the next one Samuel, an' hum only three when he fell un tull the tub o' hot watter an' was plain cooked tull death. Ut all come, I tell you, o' her wucked-headed an' foolush stubbornness. For a Samuel she must hov; an' ut was the death of the four of her sons. After the first, dudna her own mother go down un the dirt tull her feet, a-beggun' an' pleadun' wuth her no tull name her next one Samuel? But she was no tull be turned from her purpose. Margaret Henan was always set on her ways, an' never more so thon on thot name Samuel.

"She was fair lunatuc on Samuel. Dudna her neighbours' an' all kuth an' kun savun' them thot luv'd un the house wuth her, get up an' walk out ot the christenun' of the second—hum thot was cooked? Thot they dud, an' ot the very moment the munuster asked what would the bairn's name be. 'Samuel,' says she; an' wuth thot they got up an' walked out an' left the house. An' ot the door dudna her Aunt Fannie, her mother's suster, turn an' say loud for all tull hear: 'What for wull she be wantun' tull murder the wee thing?' The munuster heard fine, an' dudna like ut, but, oz he told my Larry afterward, what could he do? Ut was the woman's wush, an' there was no law again' a mother callun' her child accordun' tull her wush.

"An' then was there no the third Samuel? An' when he was lost ot sea off the Cape, dudna she break all laws o' nature tull hov a fourth? She was forty-seven, I'm tellun' ye, an' she hod a child ot forty-seven. Thunk on ut! Ot forty-seven! Ut was fair scand'lous."

From Clara, next morning, I got the tale of Margaret Henan's favourite brother; and from here and there, in the week that followed, I pieced together the tragedy of Margaret Henan. Samuel Dundee had been the youngest of Margaret's four brothers, and, as Clara told me, she had well-nigh worshipped him. He was going to sea at the time, skipper of one of the sailing ships of the Bank Line, when he married Agnes Hewitt. She was described as a slender wisp of a girl, delicately featured and with a nervous organization of the supersensitive order. Theirs had been the first marriage in the "new" church, and after a two-weeks' honeymoon Samuel had kissed his bride good-bye and sailed in command of the Loughbank, a big four-masted barque.

And it was because of the "new" church that the minister's blunder occurred. Nor was it the blunder of the minister alone, as one of the elders later explained; for it was equally the blunder of the whole Presbytery of Coughleen, which included fifteen churches on Island McGill and the mainland. The old church, beyond repair, had been torn down and the new one built on the original foundation. Looking upon the foundation-stones as similar to a ship's keel, it never entered the minister's nor the Presbytery's head that the new church was legally any other than the old church.

"An' three couples was married the first week un the new church," Clara said. "First of all, Samuel Dundee an' Agnes Hewitt; the next day Albert Mahan an' Minnie Duncan; an' by the week-end Eddie Troy and Flo Mackintosh, all sailor-men, an' un sux weeks' time the last of them back tull their ships an' awa', an' no one o' them dreamin' of the wuckedness they'd been ot."

The Imp of the Perverse must have chuckled at the situation. All things favoured. The marriages had taken place in the first week of May, and it was not till three months later that the minister, as required by law, made his quarterly report to the civil authorities in Dublin. Promptly came back the announcement that his church had no legal existence, not being registered according to the law's demands. This was overcome by prompt registration; but the marriages were not to be so easily remedied. The three sailor husbands were away, and their wives, in short, were not their wives.

"But the munster was no for alarmin' the bodies," said Clara. "He kept hus council an' bided hus time, waitun' for the lods tull be back from sea. Oz luck would have ut, he was away across the island tull a christenun' when Albert Mahan arrives home onexpected, hus shup just docked ot Dublin. Ut's nine o'clock ot night when the munster, un hus sluppers an' dressun'-gown, gets the news. Up he jumps an' calls for horse an' saddle, an' awa' he goes like the wund for Albert Mahan's. Albert uz just goun' tull bed an' hoz one shoe off when the munster arrives.

"'Come wuth me, the pair o' ye,' says he, breathless-like. 'What for, an' me dead weary an' goun' tull bed?' says Albert. 'Yull be lawful married,' says the munster. Albert looks black an' says, 'Now, munster, ye wull be jokun',' but tull humself, oz I've heard hum tell mony a time, he uz wonderun' thot the munster should a-took tull whusky ot hus time o' life.

"'We be no married?' says Minnie. He shook his head. 'An' I om no Mussus Mahan?' 'No,' says he, 'ye are no Mussus Mahan. Ye are plain Muss Duncan.' 'But ye married 'us yoursel',' says she. 'I dud an' I dudna,' says he. An' wuth thot he tells them the whole upshot, an' Albert puts on hus shoe, an' they go wuth the munster an' are married proper an' lawful, an' oz Albert Mahan says afterward mony's the time, "Tus no every mon thot hoz two weddun' nights on Island McGill.'"

Six months later Eddie Troy came home and was promptly remarried. But Samuel Dundee was away on a three-years' voyage and his ship fell overdue. Further to complicate the situation, a baby boy, past two years old, was waiting for him in the arms of his wife. The months passed, and the wife grew thin with worrying. "Ut's no meself I'm thunkun' on," she is reported to have said many times, "but ut's the puir fatherless bairn. Uf aught happened tull Samuel where wull the bairn stond?"

Lloyd's posted the Loughbank as missing, and the owners ceased the monthly remittance of Samuel's half-pay to his wife. It was the question of the child's legitimacy that preyed on her mind, and, when all hope of Samuel's return was abandoned, she drowned herself and the child in the loch. And here enters the greater tragedy. The Loughbank was not lost. By a series of sea disasters and delays too interminable to relate, she had made one of those long, unsighted passages such as occur once or twice in half a century. How the Imp must have held both his sides! Back from the sea came Samuel, and when they broke the news to him something else broke somewhere in his heart or head. Next morning they found him where he had tried to kill himself across the grave of his wife and child. Never in the history of Island McGill was there so fearful a death-bed. He spat in the minister's face and reviled him, and died blaspheming so terribly that those that tended on him did so with averted gaze and trembling hands.

And, in the face of all this, Margaret Henan named her first child Samuel.

How account for the woman's stubbornness? Or was it a morbid obsession that demanded a child of hers should be named Samuel? Her third child was a girl, named after herself, and the fourth was a boy again. Despite the strokes of fate that had already bereft her, and despite the loss of friends and relatives, she persisted in her resolve to name the child after her brother. She was shunned at church by those who had grown up with her. Her mother, after a final appeal, left her house with the warning that if the child were so named she would never speak to her again. And though the old lady lived thirty-odd years longer she kept her word. The minister agreed to christen the child any name but Samuel, and every other minister on Island McGill refused to christen it by the name she had chosen. There was talk on the part of Margaret Henan of going to law at the time, but in the end she carried the child to Belfast and there had it christened Samuel.

And then nothing happened. The whole island was confuted. The boy grew and prospered. The schoolmaster never ceased averring that it was the brightest lad he had ever seen. Samuel had a splendid constitution, a tremendous grip on life. To everybody's amazement he escaped the usual run of childish afflictions. Measles, whooping-cough and mumps knew him not. He was armour-clad against germs, immune to all disease. Headaches and earaches were things unknown. "Never so much oz a boil or a pumple," as one of the old bodies told me, ever marred his healthy skin. He broke school records in scholarship and athletics, and whipped every boy of his size or years on Island McGill.

It was a triumph for Margaret Henan. This paragon was hers, and it bore the cherished name. With the one exception of her mother, friends and relatives drifted back and acknowledged that they had been mistaken; though there were old crones who still abided by their opinion and who shook their heads ominously over their cups of tea. The boy was too wonderful to last. There was no escaping the curse of the name his mother had wickedly laid upon him. The young generation joined Margaret Henan in laughing at them, but the old crones continued to shake their heads.

Other children followed. Margaret Henan's fifth was a boy, whom she called Jamie, and in rapid succession followed three girls, Alice, Sara, and Nora, the boy Timothy, and two more girls, Florence and Katie. Katie was the last and eleventh, and Margaret Henan, at thirty-five, ceased from her exertions. She had done well by Island McGill and the Queen. Nine healthy children were hers. All prospered. It seemed her ill-luck had shot its bolt with the deaths of her first two. Nine lived, and one of them was named Samuel.

Jamie elected to follow the sea, though it was not so much a matter of election as compulsion, for the eldest sons on Island McGill remained on the land, while all other sons went to the salt-ploughing. Timothy followed Jamie, and by the time the latter had got his first command, a steamer in the Bay trade out of Cardiff, Timothy was mate of a big sailing ship. Samuel, however, did not take kindly to the soil. The farmer's life had no attraction for him. His brothers went to sea, not out of desire, but because it was the only way for them to gain their bread; and he, who had no need to go, envied them when, returned from far voyages, they sat by the kitchen fire, and told their bold tales of the wonderlands beyond the sea-rim.

Samuel became a teacher, much to his father's disgust, and even took extra certificates, going to Belfast for his examinations. When the old master retired, Samuel took over his school. Secretly, however, he studied navigation, and it was Margaret's delight when he sat by the kitchen fire, and, despite their master's tickets, tangled up his brothers in the theoretics of their profession. Tom Henan alone was outraged when Samuel, school teacher, gentleman, and heir to the Henan farm, shipped to sea before the mast. Margaret had an abiding faith in her son's star, and whatever he did she was sure was for the best. Like everything else connected with his glorious personality, there had never been known so swift a rise as in the case of Samuel. Barely with two years' sea experience before the mast, he was taken from the forecastle and made a provisional second mate. This occurred in a fever port on the West Coast, and the committee of skippers that examined him agreed that he knew more of the science of navigation than they had remembered or forgotten. Two years later he sailed from Liverpool, mate of the Starry Grace, with both master's and extra-master's tickets in his possession. And then it happened, the thing the old crones had been shaking their heads over for years.

It was told me by Gavin McNab, bos'n of the Starry Grace at the time, himself an Island McGill man.

"Wull do I remember ut," he said. "We was runnin' our Eastun' down, an' makun' heavy weather of ut. Oz fine a sailor-mon oz ever walked was Samuel Henan. I remember the look of hum wull thot last marnun', a-watch-un' them bug seas curlun' up astern, an' a-watchun' the old girl an' seeun' how she took them, the skupper down below an' drunkun' for days. Ut was ot seven thot Henan brought her up on tull the wund, not darun' tull run longer on thot fearful sea. Ot eight, after havun' breakfast, he turns un, an' a half hour after up comes the skupper, bleary-eyed an' shaky an' holdun' on tull the companion. Ut was fair smokun', I om tellun' ye, an' there he stood, blunkun' an' noddun' an' talkun' tull humsel'. 'Keep off,' says he ot last tull the mon ot the wheel. 'My God!' says the second mate, standun' beside hum. The skupper never looks tull hum ot all, but keeps on mutterun'" an' jabberun' tull humsel'. All of a suddent-like he straightens up an' throws hus head back, an' says: 'Put your wheel over, me mon—now domn ye! Are ye deef thot ye'll no be hearun' me?'

"Ut was a drunken mon's luck, for the Starry Grace wore off afore thot God-Almighty gale wuthout shuppun' a bucket o' watter, the second mate shoutun' orders an' the crew jumpun' like mod. An' wuth thot the skupper nods contented-like tull humself an' goes below after more whusky. Ut was plain murder o' the lives o' all of us, for ut was no the time for the buggest shup afloat tull be runnun'. Run? Never hov I seen the like! Ut was beyond all thunkun', an' me goun' tull sea, boy an' men, for forty year. I tell you ut was fair awesome.

"The face o' the second mate was white oz death, an' he stood ut alone for half an hour, when ut was too much for hum an' he went below an' called Samuel an' the third. Aye, a fine sailor-mon thot Samuel, but ut was too much for hum. He looked an' studied, and looked an' studied, but he could no see hus way. He durst na heave tull. She would ha' been sweeput o' all honds an' stucks an' everythung afore she could a-fetched up. There was naught tull do but keep on runnun'. An' uf ut worsened we were lost ony way, for soon or late that overtakun' sea was sure tull sweep us clear over poop an' all.

"Dud I say ut was a God-Almighty gale? Ut was worse nor thot. The devil himself must ha' hod a hond un the brewun' o' ut, ut was thot fearsome. I ha' looked on some sights, but I om no carun' tull look on the like o' thot again. No mon dared tull be un hus bunk. No, nor no mon on the decks. All honds of us stood on top the house an' held on an' watched. The three mates was on the poop, with two men ot the wheel, an' the only mon below was thot whusky-blighted captain snorun' drunk.

"An' then I see ut comun', a mile away, risun' above all the waves like an island un the sea—the buggest wave ever I looked upon. The three mates stood tulgether an' watched ut comun', a-prayun' like we thot she would no break un passun' us. But ut was no tull be. Ot the last, when she rose up like a mountain, curlun' above the stern an' blottun' out the sky, the mates scattered, the second an' third runnun' for the mizzen-shrouds an' climbun' up, but the first runnun' tull the wheel tull lend a hond. He was a brave men, thot Samuel Henan. He run straight un tull the face o' thot father o' all waves, no thunkun' on humself but thunkun' only o' the shup. The two men was lashed tull the wheel, but he would be ready tull hond un the case they was kult. An' then she took ut. We on the house could no see the poop for the thousand tons o' watter thot hod hut ut. Thot wave cleaned them out, took everythung along wuth ut—the two mates, climbun' up the mizzen-ruggun', Samuel Henan runnun' tull the wheel, the two men ot the wheel, aye, an' the wheel utself. We never saw aught o' them, for she broached tull what o' the wheel goun', an' two men o' us was drownded off the house, no tull mention the carpenter thot we pucked up ot the break o' the poop wuth every bone o' hus body broke tull he was like so much jelly."

And here enters the marvel of it, the miraculous wonder of that woman's heroic spirit. Margaret Henan was forty-seven when the news came home of the loss of Samuel; and it was not long after that the unbelievable rumour went around Island McGill. I say unbelievable. Island McGill would not believe. Doctor Hall pooh-pooh'd it. Everybody laughed at it as a good joke. They traced back the gossip to Sara Dack, servant to the Henans', and who alone lived with Margaret and her husband. But Sara Dack persisted in her assertion and was called a low-mouthed liar. One or two dared question Tom Henan himself, but beyond black looks and curses for their presumption they elicited nothing from him.

The rumour died down, and the island fell to discussing in all its ramifications the loss of the Grenoble in the China seas, with all her officers and half her crew born and married on Island McGill. But the rumour would not stay down. Sara Dack was louder in her assertions, the looks Tom Henan cast about him were blacker than ever, and Dr. Hall, after a visit to the Henan house, no longer pooh-pooh'd. Then Island McGill sat up, and there was a tremendous wagging of tongues. It was unnatural and ungodly. The like had never been heard. And when, as time passed, the truth of Sara Dack's utterances was manifest, the island folk decided, like the bos'n of the Starry Grace, that only the devil could have had a hand in so untoward a happening. And the infatuated woman, so Sara Dack reported, insisted that it would be a boy. "Eleven bairns ha' I borne," she said; "sux o' them lossies an' five o' them loddies. An' sunce there be balance un all thungs, so wull there be balance wuth me. Sux o' one an' half a dozen o' the other—there uz the balance, an' oz sure oz the sun rises un the marnun', thot sure wull ut be a boy."

And boy it was, and a prodigy. Dr. Hall raved about its unblemished perfection and massive strength, and wrote a brochure on it for the Dublin Medical Society as the most interesting case of the sort in his long career. When Sara Dack gave the babe's unbelievable weight, Island McGill refused to believe and once again called her liar. But when Doctor Hall attested that he had himself weighed it and seen it tip that very notch, Island McGill held its breath and accepted whatever report Sara Dack made of the infant's progress or appetite. And once again Margaret Henan carried a babe to Belfast and had it christened Samuel.

"Oz good oz gold ut was," said Sara Dack to me.

Sara, at the time I met her, was a buxom, phlegmatic spinster of sixty, equipped with an experience so tragic and unusual that though her tongue ran on for decades its output would still be of imperishable interest to her cronies.

"Oz good oz good," said Sara Dack. "Ut never fretted. Sut ut down un the sun by the hour an' never a sound ut would make oz long oz ut was no hungered! An' thot strong! The grup o' uts honds was like a mon's. I mind me, when ut was but hours old, ut grupped me so mighty thot I fetched a scream I was thot frightened. Ut was the punk o' health. Ut slept an' ate, an' grew. Ut never bothered. Never a night's sleep ut lost tull no one, nor ever a munut's, an' thot wuth cuttin' uts teeth an' all. An' Margaret would dandle ut on her knee an' ask was there ever so fine a loddie un the three Kungdoms.

"The way ut grew! Ut was un keepun' wuth the way ut ate. Ot a year ut was the size o' a bairn of two. Ut was slow tull walk an' talk. Exceptun' for gurgly noises un uts throat an' for creepun' on all fours, ut dudna monage much un the walkun' an' talkun' line. But thot was tull be expected from the way ut grew. Ut all went tull growun' strong an' healthy. An' even old Tom Henan cheered up ot the might of ut an' said was there ever the like o' ut un the three Kungdoms. Ut was Doctor Hall thot first suspicioned, I mind me well, though ut was luttle I dreamt what he was up tull ot the time. I seehum holdun' thungs' un fronto' luttle Sammy's eyes, an' a-makun' noises, loud an' soft, an' far an' near, un luttle Sammy's ears. An' then I see Doctor Hall go away, wrunklun' hus eyebrows an' shakun' hus head like the bairn was ailun'. But he was no ailun', oz I could swear tull, me a-seeun' hum eat an' grow. But Doctor Hall no said a word tull Margaret an' I was no for guessun' the why he was sore puzzled.

"I mind me when luttle Sammy first spoke. He was two years old an' the size of a child o five, though he could no monage the walkun' yet but went around on all fours, happy an' contented-like an' makun' no trouble oz long oz he was fed promptly, which was onusual often. I was hangun' the wash on the line ot the time when out he comes, on all fours, hus bug head waggun' tull an' fro an' blunkun' un the sun. An' then, suddent, he talked. I was thot took a-back I near died o' fright, an' fine I knew ut then, the shakun' o' Doctor Hall's head. Talked? Never a bairn on Island McGill talked so loud an' tull such purpose. There was no mustakun' ut. I stood there all tremblun' an' shakun'. Little Sammy was brayun'. I tell you, sir, he was brayun' like an ass, just like thot, loud an' long an' cheerful tull ut seemed hus lungs ud crack.

"He was a eediot, a great, awful, monster eediot. Ut was after he talked thot Doctor Hall told Margaret, but she would no believe. Ut would all come right, she said. Ut was growun' too fast for aught else. Guv ut time, said she, an' we would see. But old Tom Henan knew, an' he never held up hus head again. He could no abide the thung, an' would no brung humsel' tull touch ut, though I om no denyun' he was fair fascinated by ut. Mony the time, I see hum watchun' of ut around a corner, lookun' ot ut tull hus eyes fair bulged wuth the horror; an' when ut brayed old Tom ud stuck hus fungers tull hus ears an' look thot miserable I could a-puttied hum.

"An' bray ut could! Ut was the only thung ut could do besides eat an' grow. Whenever ut was hungry ut brayed, an' there was no stoppun' ut save wuth food. An' always of a marnun', when first ut crawled tull the kutchen-door an' blunked out ot the sun, ut brayed. An' ut was brayun' that brought about uts end.

"I mind me well. Ut was three years old an' oz bug oz a led o' ten. Old Tom hed been goun' from bed tull worse, ploughun' up an' down the fields an' talkun' an' mutterun' tull humself. On the marnun' o' the day I mind me, he was suttun' on the bench outside the kutchen, a-futtun' the handle tull a puck-axe. Unbeknown, the monster eediot crawled tull the door an' brayed after hus fashion ot the sun. I see old Tom start up an' look. An' there was the monster eediot, waggun' uts bug head an' blunkun' an' brayun' like the great bug ass ut was. Ut was too much for Tom. Somethun' went wrong wuth hum suddent-like. He jumped tull hus feet an' fetched the puck-handle down on the monster eediot's head. An' he hut ut again an' again like ut was a mod dog an' hum afeard o' ut. An' he went straight tull the stable an' hung humsel' tull a rafter. An' I was no for stoppun' on after such-like, an' I went tull stay along wuth me suster thot was married tull John Martin an' comfortable-off."

I sat on the bench by the kitchen door and regarded Margaret Henan, while with her callous thumb she pressed down the live fire of her pipe and gazed out across the twilight-sombred fields. It was the very bench Tom Henan had sat upon that last sanguinary day of life. And Margaret sat in the doorway where the monster, blinking at the sun, had so often wagged its head and brayed. We had been talking for an hour, she with that slow certitude of eternity that so befitted her; and, for the life of me, I could lay no finger on the motives that ran through the tangled warp and woof of her. Was she a martyr to Truth? Did she have it in her to worship at so abstract a shrine? Had she conceived Abstract Truth to be the one high goal of human endeavour on that day of long ago when she named her first-born Samuel? Or was hers the stubborn obstinacy of the ox? the fixity of purpose of the balky horse? the stolidity of the self-willed peasant-mind? Was it whim or fancy? the one streak of lunacy in what was otherwise an eminently rational mind? Or, reverting, was hers the spirit of a Bruno? Was she convinced of the intellectual rightness of the stand she had taken? Was hers a steady, enlightened opposition to superstition? or—and a subtler thought—was she mastered by some vaster, profounder superstition, a fetish-worship of which the Alpha and the Omega was the cryptic Samuel?

"Wull ye be tellun' me," she said, "thot uf the second Samuel hod been named Larry thot he would no hov fell un the hot watter an' drownded? Atween you an' me, sir, an' ye are untellugent-lookun' tull the eye, would the name hov made ut onyways dufferent? Would the washun' no be done thot day uf he hod been Larry or Michael? Would hot watter no be hot, an' would hot watter no burn uf he hod hod ony other name but Samuel?"

I acknowledged the justice of her contention, and she went on.

"Do a wee but of a name change the plans o' God? Do the world run by hut or muss, an' be God a weak, shully-shallyun' creature thot ud alter the fate an' destiny o' thungs because the worm Margaret Henan seen fut tull name her bairn Samuel? There be my son Jamie. He wull no sign a Rooshan-Funn un hus crew because o' believun' thot Rooshan-Funns do be monajun' the wunds an' hov the makun' o' bod weather. Wull you be thunkun' so? Wull you be thunkun' thot God thot makes the wunds tull blow wull bend Hus head from on high tull lussen tull the word o' a greasy Rooshan-Funn un some dirty shup's fo'c'sle?"

I said no, certainly not; but she was not to be set aside from pressing home the point of her argument.

"Then wull you be thunkun' thot God thot directs the stars un their courses, an' tull whose mighty foot the world uz but a footstool, wull you be thunkun' thot He wull take a spite again' Margaret Henan an' send a bug wave off the Cape tull wash her son un tull eternity, all because she was for namun' hum Samuel?"

"But why Samuel?" I asked.

"An' thot I dinna know. I wantud ut so."

"But why did you want it so?"

"An' uz ut me thot would be answerun' a such-like question? Be there ony mon luvun' or dead thot can answer? Who can tell the why o' like? My Jamie was fair daft on buttermilk, he would drunk ut tull, oz he said humself, hus back teeth was awash. But my Tumothy could no abide buttermilk. I like tull lussen tull the thunder growlun' an' roarun', an' rampajun'. My Katie could no abide the noise of ut, but must scream an' flutter an' go runnun' for the mudmost o' a feather-bed. Never yet hov I heard the answer tull the why o' like, God alone hoz thot answer. You an' me be mortal an' we canna know. Enough for us tull know what we like an' what we duslike. I like—thot uz the first word an' the last. An' behind thot like no men can go an' find the why o' ut. I like Samuel, an' I like ut well. Ut uz a sweet name, an' there be a rollun' wonder un the sound o' ut thot passes onderstandun'."

The twilight deepened, and in the silence I gazed upon that splendid dome of a forehead which time could not mar, at the width between the eyes, and at the eyes themselves—clear, out-looking, and wide-seeing. She rose to her feet with an air of dismissing me, saying—

"Ut wull be a dark walk home, an' there wull be more thon a sprunkle o' wet un the sky."

"Have you any regrets, Margaret Henan?" I asked, suddenly and without forethought.

She studied me a moment.

"Aye, thot I no ha' borne another son."

"And you would . . .?" I faltered.

"Aye, thot I would," she answered. "Ut would ha' been hus name."

I went down the dark road between the hawthorn hedges puzzling over the why of like, repeating Samuel to myself and aloud and listening to the rolling wonder in its sound that had charmed her soul and led her life in tragic places. Samuel! There was a rolling wonder in the sound. Aye, there was!

Jack London - A Short Biography

John Griffith "Jack" London was born John Griffith Chaney on January 12th 1876, near Third and Brannan Streets in San Francisco. He was directly descended from a prominent engineering family in Pennsylvania and some of the early Puritan settlers in the Massachusetts Bay Colony. Flora moved to the Pacific Coast following the death of her father, where she taught music and worked as a spiritualist. London's relationship with his father was fraught. Though the fires which followed the

1906 San Francisco earthquake destroyed his birth certificate, it is believed that his father was the astrologer William Chaney since Chaney and London's mother were living together when she became pregnant. There is strong evidence in support of this, particularly in several instances in Chaney's memoirs in which he refers to Flora as his wife, and an advertisement of Flora's for her teaching in which she refers to herself as "Florence Wellman Chaney". The claim made by Flora that Chaney demanded she have an abortion is unsubstantiated, but that shortly afterward he disclaimed responsibility for the unborn child is certain. She attempted suicide by shooting herself, though she failed and the resulting injuries left her temporarily deranged such that, on giving birth, she gave the child to Virginia Prentiss, an ex-slave, who became a prominent maternal figure for the duration of London's life. In late 1876 Flora married John London and brought her baby John wither her. As a family they settled in Oakland where London completed grade school.

By 1885 London had become an avid reader and that year he came across a copy of Signa, a lengthy Victorian novel by Ouida, which he later considered the catalyst for his literary career. He began frequenting the Oakland public library where he met Ina Coolbrith, the librarian, who actively encouraged his reading and learning through her recommendations and discussion. Later she became California's first poet laureate. He continued with this self-education until 1889 when he started work at Hickmott's Cannery, where he would often work up to eighteen hours per day. He quickly became dissatisfied with this and so borrowed money from Virginia Prentiss to buy Razzle-Dazzle, a small single-sail vessel known as a 'sloop', from an oyster pirate who was known as French Frank. Later, in his memoirs, London claimed to have stolen French Frank's mistress Mamie. The sloop lasted mere months before it was damaged beyond repair, so London turned to the California Fish Patrol for employment who hired him as a member.

In 1893 he signed on with the sealing schooner Sophie Sutherland as it was headed for Japan for several months. He returned to find the country threatened by polio, and Oakland by civil unrest brought about by labour shortage and exploitation. He found arduous work in a street-railway power plant and in a jute mill before joining Kelly's Army, a protest march formed by unemployed labourers, who would eventually march on Washington D.C. in protest. During this time as a tramp he spent thirty days in the Erie County Penitentiary in Buffalo, New York, for vagrancy. Later, in The Road, he wrote of his experience there;

Man-handling was merely one of the very minor unprintable horrors of the Erie County Pen. I say 'unprintable'; and in justice I must also say undescribable. They were unthinkable to me until I saw them, and I was no spring chicken in the ways of the world and the awful abysses of human degradation. It would take a deep plummet to reach bottom in the Erie County Pen, and I do but skim lightly and facetiously the surface of things as I there saw them.

Having completed his outstanding responsibilities with the California Fish Patrol London returned to Oakland and attended the Oakland High School, contributing numerous articles to The Aegis, the school's magazine. The first of these was "Typhoon off the Coast of Japan", in which he recounted many of his sailing experiences. During his time as a student he would frequently study at Heinold's First and Last Chance Saloon, a bar on the port in Oakland. At the age of seventeen he confided in the proprietor, John Heinold, of his ambition to go to University. Heinold loaded London the money he needed for his tuition. He particularly wanted to go to the University of California, Berkeley, and was admitted in 1896. He continued to work at Heinold's bar and during this time was introduced to several of the adventurers and sailors who would pass through Oakland, many of whom influenced his writing career, particularly Alexander McLean, a notoriously cruel sea captain who include Wolf Larsen, the protagonist in The Sea-Wolf. He was twenty-one when he enrolled at the University of California, Berkeley, and during his time there he undertook a search for the newspaper accounts of his mother's suicide attempt wherein he found the name of his biological father who by then was living in Chicago. London wrote to him eagerly, though Chaney responded by claiming impotence and that therefore he could not possibly be London's father. Moreover, on acknowledging that he had known London's mother, Chaney breezily informed London that she had been in relations with several men and that the abortion claims were slander against him. This response crushed London, and months later he quit Berkeley and headed to join the Klondike Gold Rush in the Yukon.

His time in Klondike was difficult. He, like so many others, developed various health problems as a result of malnourishment and extreme weather conditions. London suffered from scurvy, was constantly bothered by joint problems and had scars on his body and face for the rest of his life as a result of injuries and sores sustained during this period. He had left Oakland with a passing interest in social issues and, having spent much of his camp time in the Yukon in good-natured debate of matters of social interest with the wealthy Republican mining investors, returned to Oakland with an active social conscience as a socialism activist. He had also picked up some of the Republicans' capitalist ideals, realising his own intelligence and writing were his assets and that they could be exploited and nurtured in a businesslike fashion. Once back in California he wrote specifically in pursuit of publication, later detailing this experience in his 1908 novel, Martin Eden. The first work he saw published following his gold rush years was the short story To The Man On The Trail which was picked up by The Overland Monthly, though they offered him merely five dollars and were late to pay. This, he wrote later, almost ended his career, which was saved "literally and literarily" by The Black Cat, another magazine which offered forty dollars for A Thousand Deaths. That forty dollars was the first money he ever received for his writing. He eventually received his five outstanding dollars sometime afterward.

London's writing career took off in conjunction with the development of new printing technology which allowed for low-cost mass-production of popular magazines, enabling an enormous rise in the readership and popularity of these publications. In 1900 London earned approximately $2,500 from his writing, roughly $71,000 when inflation-adjusted for 2014. On April 7th of that year London married Elizabeth "Bessie" Maddern. He had known her for several years through his circle of friends and had enjoyed a strong friendship with her for much of that time. They publicly acknowledged that their marriage was out of friendship and the surety that they would produce "sturdy" children, rather than love. They shared pet-names: his for her was "Mother-Girl" and hers for him was "Daddy-Boy". On 15th January 1901 they had their first child, Joan, and a second, Bessie, on October 20th 1902. By 1903 the couple were "extremely incompatible", though London remained kind and gentle towards his wife, though he would confide in his friends privately, saying

[Bessie] is devoted to purity. When I tell her morality is only evidence of low blood pressure, she hates me. She'd sell me and the children out for her damned purity. It's terrible. Every time I come back after being away from home for a night she won't let me be in the same room with her if she can help it.

It has been suggested that part of Bessie's concerns were based on a fear that London had been "away from home for a night" visiting whores and that one day he would return carrying venereal disease.

In early 1903 London sold The Call of the Wild to The Saturday Evening Post for $750, and later the book rights to Macmillan for a further $2,000. Macmillan conducted an efficient and effective marketing campaign which saw the book sell in huge numbers. It addressed London's belief that the behaviour of animals is a direct result of the treatment they receive by their handlers and owners, something he witnessed first hand in the relationships between humans and animals in the Yukon. On July 24th 1903 London told Bessie that he was moving out, and rented a villa on Lake Merritt in Oakland. Here he met the poet George Stirling and struck up an immediate friendship. In their correspondence London signed himself as "Wolf", perhaps indicating his affinity to the animal and its wildness. With this in mind his remarks on the treatment of animals by their handlers can be seen as parallel to his own experience of his father, and that his abandonment at birth, and later personal disownment, perhaps caused London's sense of kinship with the wolf's wild existence.

The San Francisco Examiner offered London an assignment covering the Russo-Japanese War and he arrived in Yokohama on the 25th January 1904. He was quickly arrested by Japanese authorities in Shimonoseki, but thanks to American Ambassador Lloyd Griscom's intervention was soon released. He then travelled to Korea where he was soon arrested again, this time for unacceptable unauthorised proximity to the Manchuria border, and was sent back to Seoul. Once granted permission to travel to the border with the Imperial Japanese Army to observe the battle of the Yalu he continued with his assignment, though considered himself too restricted and monitored. He applied to William Randolph Hearst, the owner of the Examiner, for permission for a transfer to the Imperial Russian Army where he hoped for increased journalistic freedom. During the arrangements for this he accused his Japanese chaperones of stealing his horse's fodder which resulted in violence and his third arrest in four months. This time his release was secured by the intervention of President Theodore Roosevelt and London returned to America in June of the same year. On the 18th of August London and Stirling went to the Bohemian Grove where he was elected to honour membership of the Bohemian Club. During the whole of 1904 he and Bessie negotiated terms of a divorce which was granted on 11th November of that year.

London was introduced to Charmian Kittredge by the publisher George Platt Brett, Sr., while she was working as his secretary. They married on the 19th November 1905. Together they travelled extensively and several of their experiences would inspire his writing, particularly their time in Hawaii and Australia. London pet-named Charmian "Mate-Woman", indicating her uninhibited sexuality which was a complete contrast from his first wife Bessie. With Charmian they tried twice for a baby, suffering the death of the first at birth and the miscarriage of the second. In 1905 London bought a ranch in Glen Ellen, California, saying "next to my wife, the ranch is the dearest thing in the world to me." Though he was desperate for the ranch to be a commercial success to the extent that he considered his writing now simply a means of funding his enterprise ("I write for no other purpose than to add to the beauty that now belongs to me. I wrote a book for no other reason than to add three or four hundred acres to my magnificent estate"), it was an abject economic failure. Critics are divided over whether this is because his ranching techniques were ahead of their time (he owned the first concrete silo in California) or whether he was impaired by his alcoholism and grandiose attitude to being a ranch-owner ("London's workers laughed at his efforts to play big-time rancher [and considered] the operation a rich man's hobby"). He built an $81,000 ($2,100,000 in 2014) property named Wolf House with 26 bedrooms over 15,000 square feet which burnt down just two weeks before he and his wife were due to move in.

His literary legacy is broad, and his social legacy even broader. Accusations of racism have been levelled at him, particularly for his opinions on the increasing population and domesticity of Asia, which he detailed in a 1904 essay named "The Yellow Peril". However, he admits "it must be taken into consideration that the above postulate is itself a product of Western race-egotism, urged by our belief in our own righteousness and fostered by a faith in ourselves which may be as erroneous as are most fond race fancies." George Orwell recognised "his love of violence and physical strength, his belief in 'natural aristocracy', his animal-worship and exaltation of the primitive, he had in him what one might fairly call a Fascist strain". That 'natural aristocracy' and exaltation of the primitive can be found as a common theme throughout his life and is perhaps most informed by his childhood and relationship with his father.

London died on the 22nd of November, 1916, in the sleeping porch of one of his ranch's cottages. He had suffered several illnesses deriving from his time in the Klondike and at the time of his death had dysentery, uraemia and late stage alcoholism. He was taking morphine as pain relief and it is possible that his death was a result of an overdose. He was cremated according to his wishes and buried under a rock taken from the ruins of Wolf House.

Jack London – A Concise Bibliography

Novels
The Cruise of the Dazzler (1902)
A Daughter of the Snows (1902)
The Call of the Wild (1903)
The Kempton-Wace Letters (1903) (written with Anna Strunsky)
The Sea-Wolf (1904)
The Game (1905)
White Fang (1906)
Before Adam (1907)
The Iron Heel (1908)
Martin Eden (1909)
Burning Daylight (1910)
Adventure (1911)
The Scarlet Plague (1912)
A Son of the Sun (1912)
The Abysmal Brute (1913)
The Valley of the Moon (1913)
The Mutiny of the Elsinore (1914)
The Star Rover (1915) (published in England as The Jacket)
The Little Lady of the Big House (1916)
Jerry of the Islands (1917)
Michael, Brother of Jerry (1917)
Hearts of Three (1920) (novelization of a script by Charles Goddard)
The Assassination Bureau, Ltd (1963) (un-finished, completed by Robert L. Fish)

Short Story Collections
Son of the Wolf (1900)
Chris Farrington, Able Seaman (1901)
The God of His Fathers & Other Stories (1901)
Children of the Frost (1902)
The Faith of Men and Other Stories (1904)
Tales of the Fish Patrol (1906)
Moon-Face and Other Stories (1906)
Love of Life and Other Stories (1907)
Lost Face (1910)
South Sea Tales (1911)
When God Laughs and Other Stories (1911)
The House of Pride & Other Tales of Hawaii (1912)
Smoke Bellew (1912)
A Son of the Sun (1912)
The Night Born (1913)

The Strength of the Strong (1914)
The Turtles of Tasman (1916)
The Human Drift (1917)
The Red One (1918)
On the Makaloa Mat (1919)
Dutch Courage & Other Stories (1922)

Autobiographical Memoirs
The Road (1907)
The Cruise of the Snark (1911)
John Barleycorn (1913)

Non-Fiction & Essays
Through The Rapids On The Way To The Klondike (1899)
From Dawson To The Sea (1899)
What Communities Lose By The Competitive System (1900)
The Impossibility Of War (1900)
Phenomena Of Literary Evolution (1900)
A Letter To Houghton Mifflin Co. (1900)
Husky, Wolf Dog Of The North (1900)
Editorial Crimes – A Protest (1901)
Again The Literary Aspirant (1902)
The People of the Abyss (1903)
How I Became a Socialist (1903)[85]
The War of the Classes (1905)[84]
The Story Of An Eyewitness (1906)
A Letter To Woman's Home Companion (1906)
Revolution, and other Essays (1910)
Mexico's Army And Ours (1914)
Lawgivers (1914)
Our Adventures In Tampico (1914)
Stalking The Pestilence (1914)
The Red Game Of War (1914)
The Trouble Makers Of Mexico (1914)
With Funston's Men (1914)

Plays
"The Return of Ulysses – A Modern Version."
One-Act Play written in heroic couplets.
"The Great Interrogation." One-Act Play, written with Lee Bascom (1905)
"As It Was in the Beginning." A Four-Act Comedy, written with Lee Bascom (1905)
Scorn of Women (1906). A Three-Act Play.
"Gold." A Three-Act Play, written with Herbert Heron (1910)
"Billy the Kid." (1910)
Theft (1910). A Four-Act Play.
The First Poet (1911). A One-Act Play.
"War." A Drama of Peace in Three Acts, written with Joseph Noel. (1912. Unpublished)
"Babylonia," A Musical Comedy, written with C. P. Clement and Edward Gage (1913. Unpublished)
"Gold." A Three-Act Play, written with Herbert Heron. (1913)
"The Damascus Road." A Three-Act Play, written with Walter H. Nichols, first as "The Common Man,"
and revised as "The Damascus Road." (1913. Unpublished)

"Daughters of the Rich," One-Act Play. (1915)
The Acorn Planter. A Three-Act Play (1916)
The Birth Mark (1917). A One-Act Play.
A Wicked Woman (1917) A One-Act Play.

Poetry
A Heart
Abalone Song (1913)
And Some Night (1914)
Ballade Of The False Lover (1914)
Cupid's Deal (1913)
Daybreak (1901)
Effusion (1901)
George Sterling (1913)
Gold (1915)
He Chortled With Glee (1899)
He Never Tried Again (1912)
His Trip To Hades (1913)
Homeland (1914)
Hors De Saison (1913)
If I Were God (1899)
In A Year (1901)
In And Out (1911)
Je Rls En Espoir (1914)
Memory (1913)
Moods (1913)
My Confession (1912)
My Little Palmist (1914)
Of Man Of The Future (1915)
Oh You Everybody's Girl (19)
On The Face Of The Earth You Are The One (1915)
Rainbows End (1914)
Republican Rallying Song (1916)
Sonnet (1901)
The Gift Of God (1905)
The Klondyker's Dream (1914)
The Lover's Liturgy (1913)
The Mammon Worshippers (1911)
The Republican Battle-Hymn (1905)
The Return Of Ulysses (1915)
The Sea Sprite And The Shooting Star (1916)
The Socialist's Dream (1912)
The Song Of The Flames (1903)
The Way Of War (1906)
The Worker And The Tramp (1911)
Tick! Tick! Tick! (1915)
Too Late (1912)
Weasel Thieves (1913)
When All The World Shouted My Name (1905)
Where The Rainbow Fell (1902)
Your Kiss (1914)

Short Stories

An Old Soldier's Story (1894)
Who Believes in Ghosts! (1895)
And 'FRISCO Kid Came Back (1895)
Night's Swim In Yeddo Bay (1895)
One More Unfortunate (1895)
Sakaicho, Hona Asi And Hakadaki (1895)
A Klondike Christmas (1897)
Mahatma's Little Joke (1897)
O Haru (1897)
Plague Ship (1897)
The Strange Experience Of A Misogynist (1897)
Two Gold Bricks (1897)
The Devil's Dice Box (1898)
A Dream Image (1898)
The Test: A Clondyke Wooing (1898)
To the Man on Trail (1898)
In a Far Country (1899)
The King of Mazy May (1899)
The End Of The Chapter (1899)
The Grilling Of Loren Ellery (1899)
The Handsome Cabin Boy (1899)
In The Time Of Prince Charley (1899)
Old Baldy (1899)
The Men of Forty Mile (1899)
Pluck And Pertinacity (1899)
The Rejuvenation of Major Rathbone (1899)
The White Silence (1899)
A Thousand Deaths (1899)
Wisdom of the Trail (1899)
An Odyssey of the North (1900)
The Son of the Wolf (1900)
Even unto Death (1900)
The Man with the Gash (1900)
A Lesson In Heraldry (1900)
A Northland Miracle (1900)
Proper "GIRLIE" (1900)
Thanksgiving On Slav Creek (1900)
Their Alcove (1900)
Housekeeping In The Klondike (1900)
Dutch Courage (1900)
Where the Trail Forks (1900)
Hyperborean Brew (1901)
A Relic of the Pliocene (1901)
The Lost Poacher" (1901)
The God of His Fathers (1901)
FRISCO Kid's "Story" (1901)
The Law of Life (1901)
The Minions of Midas (1901)
In the Forests of the North (1902)

The "Fuzziness" of Hoockla-Heen (1902)
The Story of Keesh (1902)
Keesh, Son of Keesh (1902)
Nam-Bok, the Unveracious (1902)
Li Wan the Fair (1902)
Lost Face
Master of Mystery (1902)
The Sunlanders (1902)
The Death of Ligoun (1902)
Moon-Face (1902)
Diable—A Dog (1902), renamed Bâtard in 1904
To Build a Fire (1902, revised 1908)
The League of the Old Men (1902)
The Dominant Primordial Beast (1903)
The One Thousand Dozen (1903)
The Marriage of Lit-lit (1903)
The Shadow and the Flash (1903)
The Leopard Man's Story (1903)
Negore the Coward (1904)
All Gold Cañon (1905)
Love of Life" (1905)
The Sun-Dog Trail" (1905)
The Apostate (1906)
Up The Slide (1906)
Planchette (1906)
Brown Wolf (1906)
Make Westing (1907)
Chased By The Trail (1907)
Trust (1908)
A Curious Fragment (1908)
Aloha Oe (1908)
That Spot (1908)
The Enemy of All the World (1908)
The Heathen (1908)
The House of Mapuhi (1909)
Good-by, Jack (1909)
Samuel (1909)
South of the Slot (1909)
The Chinago (1909)
The Dream of Debs (1909)
The Madness of John Harned (1909)
The Seed of McCoy (1909)
A Piece of Steak (1909)
Mauki (1909)
Goliath (1910)
The Unparalleled Invasion (1910)
Told in the Drooling Ward (1910)
When the World was Young (1910)
The Terrible Solomons (1910)
The Inevitable White Man (1910)
Yah! Yah! Yah! (1910)

By the Turtles of Tasman (1911)
The Mexican (1911)
War (1911)
The Unmasking Of The Cad (1911)
The Scarlet Plague (1912)
The Captain Of The Susan Drew (1912)
The Sea-Farmer (1912)
The Feathers of the Sun (1912)
The Prodigal Father (1912)
Samuel (1913)
The Sea-Gangsters (1913)
The Strength of the Strong (1914)
Told in the Drooling Ward (1914)
The Hussy (1916)
Like Argus of the Ancient Times (1917)
Jerry of the Islands (1917)
The Red One (1918)
Shin-Bones (1918)
The Bones of Kahekili (1919)

www.ingramcontent.com/pod-product-compliance
Lightning Source LLC
Chambersburg PA
CBHW070943200626
46811CB00025B/1478